A FOOL FOR A CLIENT

A FOOL FOR A CLIENT

PARNELL HALL

PEGASUS CRIME
NEW YORK LONDON

A FOOL FOR A CLIENT

Pegasus Books LLC
80 Broad Street, 5th Floor
New York, NY 10004

First Pegasus Books cloth edition October 2015

Interior design by Maria Fernandez

ISBN: 978-1-60598-883-2

10 9 8 7 6 5 4 3 2 1

Printed in the United States of America
Distributed by W. W. Norton & Company, Inc.

For Jim and Franny

1

"I have a fool for a client."

I didn't doubt it. Richard Rosenberg was one of New York City's top negligence lawyers, with literally thousands of clients, so it was not surprising that one them should happen to be foolish, particularly since the people who hired an attorney who advertised on TV tended to be less than affluent, less than well connected, and inevitably less than intelligent. Richard didn't have to tell me he had a fool for a client. Having signed up over half of them myself, I could attest to the fact he had several.

"You want me to talk to him, Richard?" I said.

Richard frowned. "Don't try to be funny. I was trying to be funny. Did you really not get it? Don't tell me you're not familiar with that old saw? Let me begin again. I have a fool for an *investigator.*"

"Richard—"

"A lawyer who represents himself has a fool for a client!" Richard said. "Can you *possibly* not know that?"

"You're the client?"

"Sorry. Bonus round is over. You get no credit. Yes, I'm the client. It's not bad enough I'm in trouble, I don't even get to joke about it."

"You're in trouble?"

"No, I fell going into my office and I'm suing myself for negligence. I'm my own client and my own defendant. The only issue now is whether I can represent myself against myself. It will certainly expedite things if I'm the attorney on both sides of the suit."

Richard's sarcasm was legendary. His summaries to the jury were often quoted to first-year law students. A little man with a boundless source of nervous energy, Richard wore opposing counsel down through a barrage of whatever leapt like lighting into his diabolically brilliant mind. In such summations he had been known to talk for five minutes straight without ever coming near whatever the hell it was he was supposed to be talking about, until most jurors had lost track of the case they were trying and reasoned the sheer genius of what they had just heard could not possibly be wrong.

But even on those occasions he would eventually get to the punch line. I hoped he would here.

"I'm at sea, Richard. Who are you trying to sue?"

"Sue?" Richard rolled his eyes. "Stanley, it's not a civil case."

"It's a criminal case?"

"Yes."

"You're the defendant?"

"Didn't I say that?"

"What's the charge?"

Richard sighed. "Murder."

I sat up straight in my chair. It was not easy to do. The comfortable overstuffed chair Richard had placed opposite his desk was for the purpose of relaxing clients on the one hand and making opposing counsel feel small and helpless on the other. It was tough to sit up on the edge. Opponents in the know often pulled up a folding chair or opted to stand.

"Richard, I don't want to spoil your fun, but could you tell me what this is all about?"

Richard groaned. "You can't even do that right. There's no surer way to spoil someone's fun than by saying I don't want to spoil your fun."

"You're charged with murder?"

"I will be."

"Why?"

"I supposedly killed my girlfriend."

"You have a girlfriend?"

"Not anymore." He put up his hand. "Sorry. Bad joke. Yes, I had a girlfriend. Maybe that's too strong a word. We'd been going out for a while. Her name's Jeannie Atkins. She was a divorcée, worked as a law clerk for Judge Peters."

"Judge Peters? You were dating Judge Peters's law clerk? Isn't that a conflict of interest?"

Richard shook his head. "See, *that* point of law you know. Yes, it might have been a conflict of interest, but Judge Peters doesn't do negligence work."

I knew that. Judge Peters did criminal work, usually high-profile cases of a sensational nature, which is why I knew the name. "He's not handling this?"

"I don't know who's handling this, but it wouldn't be him. He'd recuse himself. He's doing Global Banking, anyway."

Global Banking was a case on the magnitude of Tyco or Enron. Clearly he wouldn't be free for a while.

"So when was she killed?"

"Last night."

"How did it happen?"

"How do the police *think* it happened, or how did it *really* happen?"

"Do you *know* how it happened?"

"No."

"What *do* you know?"

"She was killed last night, most likely between midnight and one A.M."

"Were you there?"

"Not when she was killed."

"Why do the police think you were?"

"Because they're morons."

"Besides that."

"I was the last person to see her alive."

"What about the killer?"

"He was the first person to see her dead."

My mouth fell open. "You can joke about it?"

"I'm in shock, Stanley. Someone I cared about is dead. Inexplicably—well, maybe not inexplicably—the police think I had something to do with it. I have an acute legal mind, I'm used to rolling with the punches and handling any situation. And I'm utterly lost. I am shaken, and I feel like my fucking head is coming off."

Richard paused. His face looked utterly drained. "And I'm scared. Really scared. Something has happened that I can't handle. It's personal. And it's the first time it's ever been personal. I don't feel like I'm up to it."

"Why don't you hire a lawyer?"

"I don't *trust* lawyers! They're a sleazy bunch of scum-sucking, bottom-feeding opportunists, perverting the law to further their own interests! There's not one of them I would trust not to sell me out for a nickel!"

"*You're* a lawyer."

"I rest my case."

It was as human a moment as I'd ever seen from Richard. Like he'd let down all his defenses and laid his soul bare. It must have embarrassed him utterly, because he'd covered immediately with his diatribe about lawyers. Which I played into, setting him up with *you're a lawyer* so he could bounce back into repartee with *I rest my case.*

I hoped, having gotten all that out of the way, he'd be able to relax and tell his story.

He was.

3

"Last night we were out on a date. I took her out to dinner. Peter Luger's, you know it?"

I knew *of* it. I'd never been there. New York City's most famous steak house was out of my price range. It was also out of my neighborhood. Peter Luger's is in Brooklyn, you have to make reservations years in advance, and you don't order off the menu, you just tell the waiter how many people and he brings you your steak. Well-to-do big eaters often inflate that number—a couple will order steak for three or even four.

My wife and I sometimes order Thai food for two. It's delivered right to our door.

"That's in Brooklyn, right?"

"Yeah."

"How'd you get there?"

"Car service."

"Limo was in the shop?"

"I don't *have* a limo. I wasn't going to take my date on the subway. I hired a car service."

"How'd you get home?"

"Car service."

"You called another?"

"Same one."

"You had them wait?"

"That's what they're paid for."

"What time was that?"

"Nine-thirty. Maybe a little before. I made a reservation for seven. It was a leisurely dinner. We lingered over cognac. Then I drove her back to her apartment."

"Where's that?"

"Fifth Avenue and Seventy-seventh."

"Nice."

"Just a small one-bedroom."

"You pay for it?"

"No, I don't pay for it. She got a nice divorce settlement."

"You handled the divorce?"

"I don't do divorce work."

"So what time did you drop her off at her apartment?"

"Around ten."

"You went in?"

"Just to say goodnight."

"What time did you leave?"

"Around eleven."

"You took your time saying goodnight."

"I was looking for just the right words."

"So you left at eleven?"

"Eleven. Eleven-fifteen."

"How'd you get home?"

"Car service."

"He waited for you?"

"Yeah."

I sighed. "So what'd you tell the cops?"

"I told them to go fuck themselves. I'm a lawyer, Stanley. I told 'em I know damn well I have the right to remain silent, and I'm exercising that right. Charge me or release me, and hurry up about it, I got a law practice to run."

"You didn't tell 'em anything?"

"Of course not. I may have a fool for a client, but luckily that fool's got a hell of a lawyer."

"So what do you want me to do?"

"I would like to know about the case. Unfortunately, no one will tell me about the case because I'm the client so I can't talk about the case. You, on the other hand, are not the client."

"Richard—"

"You are an investigator hired by the attorney to dig out information for the client. You can talk to anybody and it will not reflect upon the client because you will not be making damaging admissions that can be used against the client in the event of a trial."

"And what sort of investigations did you have in mind?"

"Well, it would be nice to know what the police have. And not just because I might be accused of the crime. I'm upset. I want to know who did it, and I want to make damn sure the police don't pick the wrong guy, whether they pick on me or whether they pick on some other poor schmuck who didn't actually do it."

"And how do you expect me to find out?"

"Well, we need an inside track. We need to know what's happening."

"You want me to talk to MacAullif."

"Well, you know MacAullif."

"You want me to abuse my friendship with MacAullif to get him to tell us something."

"That's not the way it is."

"That's the way he'll see it."

Sergeant MacAullif scowled. "You want to abuse my friendship and get the inside dope on the Atkins murder?"

"I told Richard that was how you'd see it."

"Richard asked you to abuse my friendship?"

"Richard insisted you wouldn't see it that way."

"Richard's a lawyer. He'll claim up is down and make it sound good. He's bent out of shape because someone bumped off his girl-friend. So he wants to play martyr and avenging angel all at once. So he sends his ace investigator out to pump the cops."

"You don't think he did it?"

"Not unless he grew a pair of balls. Can you imagine him killing anyone?"

"No. Can you?"

"I can't imagine him *fucking* anyone. But someone was. If it's not him, he's got nothing to worry about. Except looking like a wimp when it comes out."

"You're all heart, MacAullif."

"Not according to my cardiologist. I got hardening of the arteries, thickening of the heart wall. To hear the guy go on, you'd think I'm a flight of stairs away from bypass. I cut down on the beer, the weight is under control—well, maybe not." MacAullif jerked open his desk drawer, took out a pair of cigars, began drumming them on the desk. That was a good sign. He didn't smoke them anymore, but he played with cigars when he was talking something out. As if he didn't get rid of a little nervous energy, heads were going to roll.

He jerked open another drawer, took out a file, flipped a page. "Somebody fucked the broad. She had semen in her." MacAullif squinted closer at the report. "No, that's semen *on* her. So it might have been a hand job. Or a blow job that wasn't swallowed."

I tried to crowd the images out of my head. It was hard to reconcile them with Richard.

MacAullif flipped a page. "Decedent was due for a deposition this morning, didn't show up. When she didn't answer the phone, they sent the super up to check. He went in with a passkey and found her. She was stark naked, hacked to pieces with a steak knife from her kitchen. The body was spread-eagled on her bed. Blood was everywhere. The coroner puts the time of death most likely between eleven and one A.M."

"Outside of a snuff film, who takes a steak knife to bed with a woman?"

"You watch snuff films?"

"I've *heard* of snuff films. Don't get sidetracked."

"I don't know how you get someone in bed naked with a steak knife. Hold 'em at knifepoint and tell 'em to take their clothes off?"

"I don't know, MacAullif."

"It seems a radical approach."

"How'd they get on to Richard so fast?"

"Car service gave him up. Driver thought he recognized her picture on TV."

"Great."

"According to the driver, Richard came out 11:45 and he drove him home."

"11:45?"

"Yeah."

"Sure it was that late?"

"According to the report."

"So Richard came out at 11:45."

"Yeah, why?"

"That's not good."

"No shit. It's a wonder he's out walking around. Apparently he's got a hell of an attorney."

"So when he came out, did he seem agitated?"

"How the hell should I know?"

"You got the report."

"It isn't in the report."

"Anything about his manner? How he seemed?"

"No."

"Well, was he covered in blood?"

"There's no mention of it."

"That's the kind of detail a cop would be apt to include."

"You'd think."

"Well, what kind of details are there?"

"None. Other than he came out and the guy drove him home."

"Did he say anything on the ride?"

"If he did, it didn't make the report."

"Got the driver's name?"

MacAullif looked up from the paper. "See, this is where I get fucked every time. I'm a nice guy, give you what I got. Then you ask me for some totally innocuous something or other that means I'm in a world of shit. If you go talk to the driver it's gonna blow up in your face, you're gonna get hauled in for meddling in a police investigation, and they're gonna wanna know where you got your lead."

"MacAullif, calm down. Richard hired the fucking car. You are not the only source of the information. I could find out the guy's name just by calling the car service."

"They might not give it to you."

"Are you telling me the police would have told the car service to withhold vital information from the defendant?"

"Are you asking to be thrown out on your ear?"

"No, I'm just pointing out if the police make it hard for me to get the information, I will get it another way. Of course when I do, the cops will think you gave it to me, but there's nothing I can do about that."

"God save me from a wiseass." MacAullif picked up the sheet again. "The guy's name is Freddie Baldar. Would you like his address and phone number?"

"I was hoping for his astrological sign."

MacAullif read off the address. I copied it into my notebook.

"Anything else I can get you?"

"What else have you got?"

"I got a hot tip. Attorneys don't like Richard Rosenberg much. He's a smug son of a bitch, makes 'em look bad in court. There's a bunch of ADAs just waiting for him to trip on his dick. I don't know which one will get assigned to this case, but I think you can count on a fairly zealous prosecution."

"What about the doorman?"

"Doorman?"

"A Fifth Avenue apartment, surely they have a doorman."

"They don't mention one."

"Why wouldn't they take a statement from the doorman, identify Richard as the man who went up to her apartment?"

"That's fairly well established by the driver."

"He didn't go in. For all he knows, Richard hung out in the lobby for two hours."

"They're not building a case in court. They're investigating the crime."

"Oh, you think it's the ADA who goes out and finds the doorman?"

"No, I think the cops do. It doesn't happen to be in this file, but they just got the case. Doubtless they've interviewed the doorman by now but didn't feel the need to inform me. I'm sure if they knew you were dropping by for an update, they'd have faxed it over."

"Oh, thank you. Richard was understandably off his game, so it's good to get my daily requirement of sarcasm."

"It's good to get mine," MacAullif said. "It takes my mind off the four homicides I have pending. None of which happens to be this one."

"You don't have the case?"

"If I had the case, don't you think I'd know a little more than I know now?"

"You might have it and just not tell me."

"It's good you know that."

"But that's not the situation."

"How do you know that?"

"You told me it isn't your case. You wouldn't tell me that if it was. You'd deflect the question. Manage not to answer. But you wouldn't lie. You tell me flat out it's not yours, I can take that to the bank."

"I'll remember that the next time I want to trick you."

"Won't work. I'm on to you now," I stood up. "Listen, this is a lot of fun, but my boss is in trouble. If this isn't your case, whose is it?"

"Oh."

That's all he had to say.

Two thoughts occurred to me just then. One was that I knew MacAullif entirely too well if that single syllable could convey so much information.

The other was that Richard's troubles, which had seemed insurmountable, had just escalated geometrically.

"Don't tell me," I said, hoping against hope that I was wrong, though in my heart of hearts I knew that it was true.

MacAullif sighed. "Yeah. I hate to be the one to tell you, but Richard's totally fucked."

He nodded. "It's Sergeant Thurman."

5

There are all kinds of cops. There are good cops and bad cops. There are smart cops and dumb cops. There are thin cops and fat cops. There are old cops and young cops. And uniformed cops and plainclothes cops. And desk cops and beat cops and undercover cops. And cops who get letters of commendation and cops who toss service weapons and shields on desks.

Sergeant Thurman had his own special category.

Cops you wouldn't turn to if being chased down the street by machete-waving maniacs.

Sergeant Thurman had raised incompetence to an art form.

His office reflected the man himself. It would have reflected him more had the walls been capable of bulging out. That's not to say that Sergeant Thurman was fat. He was big, stocky, solidly built, carved from granite, particularly between the ears. But that's unfair. The man had thoughts. They just usually managed to ignore reality.

Thurman's desk was stacked with files, though stacked perhaps implies too much organization. Pending files were strewn along with nonpending files, papers that had never been filed, reports that had never been written, daily newspapers, takeout menus, and, most likely, evidence that had been mislaid. Which is a polite euphemism for hidden from the defense.

Not that Sergeant Thurman was crooked. Let me not demean the man. He was a straight shooter who would no sooner frame an innocent man than he would let a guilty one escape. Unfortunately, he had trouble telling the difference. And once he got it in his head that you were guilty, anything was fair game. He was not framing an innocent man, he was ensuring the conviction of a guilty one. And if that required the manipulation of the evidence, well, it was all in the cause of justice.

I had had run-ins with Sergeant Thurman in the past. When he'd been out to get me, it was bad. When he wanted to help me, it was worse.

I found the good sergeant in his office, chewing out a subordinate. The officer in question had apparently purchased coffee at a cart on the corner instead of the approved coffee stand. The resultant sludge was probably identical, but apparently there was a monetary difference of ten cents a cup.

I waited until Thurman had made a telling point, then cut in before he could formulate another devastating zinger.

His eyes lit up when he saw me. *Lit up* is the wrong choice of words. The glimmer of recognition was doubtless the one reserved for any conscious thought. But he focused his full attention on me, and the grateful young officer escaped out the door.

"Well, well," Thurman said. "Don't I know you from somewhere?"

"Probably some arrest warrant or other."

"Yeah, that's gotta be it. Is it outstanding?"

"Well, it wasn't bad."

Thurman frowned, not getting it.

"No, it wouldn't be a pending warrant, Thurman."

"I didn't think so. Can't say the same for your boss."

"You got a warrant out on Richard?"

Thurman shrugged. "Not my call. If it was, he'd be in lockup. ADAs don't wanna touch him until it's on ice. Seems he's got a reputation. I wouldn't know about that. I know he's a slick shyster. Doesn't mean he can get away with murder."

"Richard didn't kill anyone."

"Of course you'd say that. If he goes to jail, your salary stops."

"I understand it's your case."

"Oh, you understand that, do you? Then you must know how eager I am to share it with you."

"I could think of a reason why you might be."

"Oh? What is that?"

"Like you said, you're stymied. You can't act without the ADA. I can. Gimme a lead, I'll give it back."

"I didn't say I can't act. I can't make the arrest, but I can investigate just fine. Which means you got nothing to trade."

"What if I got something you don't?"

"How would you do that?"

"Running down the leads you give me."

"That'll be hard to do when I don't give you any."

"Not as hard as you think. I know exactly what Richard did and when he did it. You got secondhand evidence. I got first. I know more than you do already."

"Like what?"

"I know the testimony of the driver and the doorman doesn't jibe."

"Says who?"

"Says me. Driver says Richard came out eleven forty-five. Doorman says it was earlier."

"Who told you that?"

"Who do you think?"

"You talk to the doorman?"

"When would I have done that?"

"I don't know, but you're tricky." Thurman jerked a file out of the mess on his desk. How he knew which one to grab I have no idea. He flipped it open, ran his finger down the page. I could practically see his lips moving. "There is no discrepancy in the time the guy left."

"Then why would I get a report that there was?"

"Who'd you get it from?"

"An anonymous tip."

"Your buddy MacAullif meddling in my case?"

"Absolutely not. He's got too many cases of his own."

"What'd he tell you about it?"

"It's not his case, you're in charge."

"Anything else?"

"Yeah, no one's telling him anything because they're afraid he'll tell me. Which is pretty stupid when you come to think of it."

"Why do you say that?"

"Richard's either guilty or he's not. If he's guilty, nothing MacAullif can say is going to hurt. If he's not, you don't wanna convict him anyway. You wanna get the guy who is."

"I've heard that argument so many times I'm sick of it. You know how many defendants get off scot free because some lawyer twisted the facts?"

"Would it be about the same as the innocent ones who go to the chair?"

"Fuck you."

I shook my head. "I'd hoped for a little cooperation."

"Are you kidding me? Why in the world would I cooperate with you?"

"I gave you a reason."

"And I told you what I thought of it. That should have ended the conversation."

"You want me to go?"

"Wow! A real Einstein. Why is a guy as sharp as you stuck in the same dead-end job?"

"I keep flunking the sergeant's exam."

That caught him up short. He didn't know what to make of it. It seemed like an insult but to whom? It was, of course, a totally meaningless bit of gibberish dreamed up expressly for the purpose of fucking with his mind.

It did. He tried to figure it out, couldn't see there was nothing to figure. Instead he reacted the way I expected he would. He threw me out of his office.

I was happy to go.

I was even happier that I'd learned how to read upside down.

6

Ramon Castella lived on the sixth floor of a six-story apartment house in Queens. The good news was it had an elevator. The bad news was everything else. It had chipped paint—probably lead—peeling off the walls. It had water on the floor that smelled suspiciously like it had leaked from a sewage pipe. And it had a rat. Probably more than one, but there was one that I could see. It eyed me suspiciously as I crossed the lobby. Clearly it had a right to be there, but what the hell was I doing?

I was calling on the doorman whose address I'd read upside down in Sergeant Thurman's file. I rode the elevator up to his floor, heaved a sigh of relief when the door actually opened, and walked down the dimly lit hall to his apartment.

Ramon Castella was one of those men who always strike me as a grownup, someone older than me by virtue of their body type, dress, or personal grooming. The man had a thin mustache, beady eyes, and pointed nose. Much as some owners resembled their dogs, the doorman was practically a dead ringer for the rat in the lobby. Though probably less cordial.

"I don't know why you're bothering me," he griped. "I gave everything to the other officer."

That was a moment of truth. The word *other* had raised the conversation to another level. Failing to disillusion Mr. Castella would make the difference between being a pain-in-the-ass meddling private eye and impersonating a police officer. The former risked no jail time. The latter practically begged for it.

Unfortunately, disillusioning Mr. Castella was apt to end the conversation. The best I could hope for was the guy wouldn't remember he'd said *other*. I pushed by him into the room as if I had every right to be there.

Ramon Castella's living room was dominated by a couch, a reclining chair, and a big-ass, high-definition TV. The man smoked, and his coffee table was littered with ashtrays, all of them full, and dirty coffee cups doubling for them. I had interrupted him during some favorite program or other. His DVR had frozen the picture of whatever the hell he was watching.

"I have one or two questions," I said. "You cooperate, it won't take long. You wanna argue, I'll be here a while."

Castella snorted. "Oh, for Christ's sake."

"As far as I'm concerned, your story's straightforward." I sat down, whipped out a notepad, tried to look official. "You were on duty last night at Jeannie Atkins's apartment building?"

"That's right."

"You're not on duty tonight."

"I get two days off a week. This is one of them."

"What time you get off?"

"Midnight."

"You were on last night until twelve?"

"That's right."

"Who goes on at midnight?"

"The super."

"The super mans the desk?"

"'Course he does."

"Where's his apartment?"

"Off the back hallway."

"Nice apartment?"

He seemed surprised by the question. "Yeah. For a one bedroom on the first floor, it's damn nice."

"The super married?"

"No."

"Got a girlfriend?"

"What's that got to do with anything?"

"Hey, I'm taking down names of witnesses. If she's in the building, I should know. What's her name?"

"Angela."

"Angela what?"

"I don't know. Just Angela."

"What's the super's name?"

"Tony."

"Tony what?"

"Tony Fuller."

"He comes on at twelve?"

"That's right."

"He come out and sit at the desk?"

"Why?"

I looked up from my notepad. "You know, you're asking more questions than you're answering. The point of this investigation is not to satisfy your curiosity. I'm trying to get an accurate take on what happened last night. To do that, I need to know the workings of the building. Now, when the super comes on at midnight, does he sit in the lobby or does he wait in his apartment, maybe with the door open, in case someone wants to get in?"

"I dunno. If I was him, I'd wait in my apartment."

"Could he do that?"

"What do you mean?"

"What if someone he didn't know came in?"

"They couldn't do that."

"Why not?"

"Front door's locked. Tenants get in with a key. Anyone else has to ring the bell."

"Or call upstairs and get buzzed in?"

"Not that type of building. Front door's locked, it's gotta open with a key or from the inside."

"Is the door locked while you're on duty?"

"No."

"Why not?"

"I'm in the lobby. Someone wants in, they gotta come to the desk."

"There's no other way in? A service entrance, for instance?"

He shook his head. "It's locked. And the super's got the only key. And the door's out back and through a gate that's locked and topped with razor wire."

I nodded. "How long you worked there?"

"Let's see. I been there eight years."

"So you know the system pretty well."

"That's right."

"You went off duty at midnight. You lock the front door when you left?"

"Of course I did."

"Did you see the super or did you just take off?"

"Super was there."

"In the lobby?"

"No, in his apartment."

"So you didn't see him."

"I see him all the time."

I was asking questions just to get the guy relaxed and used to answering them, but I'd clearly hit on something. He was being evasive and I didn't know why. I had visions of Ramon and the super selling drugs on the side. Which was certainly interesting but wasn't what I wanted.

It had one practical use, however. If the guy didn't want to talk about the super, he'd be happy to steer the conversation back to the matter at hand.

"So you were on the desk when Jeannie Atkins came home?"

"That's right."

"And you saw the guy who came in with her?"

"Of course."

"Did you recognize him?"

"Sure. I identified his photograph."

"You know his name?"

"I didn't then. I do now. Richard Rosenberg. Guy's a lawyer, for Christ's sake. You'd think he'd know better."

"Had you seen him before?"

"Oh, sure. Quite a few times. Figured he was the boyfriend. Guess he was, you know, to get that angry."

"And did you see him leave?"

"Sure."

"And what time was that?"

"Quarter to twelve."

"Why'd you notice the time?"

He shrugged. "That's my job."

"Yeah, but it's not like you have to clock people in and out. They don't *sign* in and out, do they?"

"Of course not."

"So when you say a quarter to twelve, that's an approximation."

"Whose side are you on? I saw the guy go out, it was a quarter to twelve. I don't know what to tell you."

"You went off duty right after that?"

"Not right after. At midnight."

"So it wasn't right before you went off duty?"

"Fifteen minutes."

"At twelve o'clock you locked the door and went home?"

"That's right."

"Was the super in the lobby?"

He scowled. "You tryin' to get the super in trouble? He does his job. Midnight he's on. And I don't want you sayin' anything different, you understand?"

"You don't want him to think you told on him."

"There's nothing to tell. I went off, he went on, end of story."

"I understand. I'm just trying to get it straight."

"Well, it's straight. And what difference does it make? The guy was gone by then anyway."

"Right," I said. "So, when this Rosenberg character came out, what was he like?"

"What do you mean?"

"Well, if he just killed someone, you'd expect it to show. He'd be agitated. Upset. Maybe his clothes would be mussed from the struggle."

"His clothes were often mussed, you know what I mean?"

I did, and I didn't appreciate the way he turned the conversation. "Anything out of the ordinary. Like a trace of blood?"

"You don't think I'd have mentioned that?"

"No, I think you would. That's why it's significant that you didn't."

He peered at me quizzically. "You're claiming the guy might get away if I don't say there was blood?"

"Don't be silly. No one's asking you to lie, no one's asking you to say anything that isn't true. All I wanna know is the facts. We gotta know what they are before the case goes to trial. There can't be any surprises in the courtroom."

"Yeah, well, I gave you all I have. I saw him go in, and I saw him go out."

"And did anyone else come to see her while you were on duty?"

"No, they didn't."

"So, between the time she got home and midnight, when you went off duty, no one came to see her?"

He hesitated.

"You thought of something?"

He was instantly angry. "No, I didn't think of something. It's just the way you said it. Putting words in my mouth. 'No one came to see her.' No one came by the *desk*. Someone who lived in the building could have seen her. Or someone could have gone in to see somebody else and stopped in to see her on the way out."

"You think that happened?"

"No, I don't think that happened. I mean, Jesus Christ, you're a pain in the ass. You tell me no one could have seen her, like that's what I said. That's *not* what I said. I said no one came by the desk. You and the other cop start comparing notes and say, 'You said this to him you said that to me, which is it,' I am going to be pissed. I understand I gotta be a witness, but, for Christ's sake, I'm not on trial."

I wasn't happy about him referring to the other cop again. If the police reinterviewed him, I wouldn't want him referring to *me* as the other cop. I figured if I left it alone, I could always come back. Not that there was likely to be any need.

I hung it up, drove back to Manhattan.

I was pretty depressed. I hadn't found out a thing.

And Richard was beginning to look guilty.

7

"Did he do it?"

I gawked at my wife in surprise. "Alice, how can you ask me that?"

"Well, it seems a relevant question. It might influence how you approach the case."

"Alice, can you imagine Richard killing someone?"

"Stanley, it's sex. People get crazed over sex."

My mouth hung open. Alice has no sympathy at all when I get crazed over sex. "What do you mean?"

"Well, if he was jealous, if it turned out she was seeing someone else, or decided to dump him and told him that."

"There was semen involved."

"What's your point?"

"You think they had sex and she said get the fuck out of here?"

"She might have phrased it better."

Alice was looking good in one of my pocket t-shirts over what was obviously nothing. Let me rephrase that. Over what was obviously no underclothing. Anyway, I admired the result. My old pocket-t had never looked better.

"What's MacAullif say?"

"Says it's not his case."

"Yeah, it's Thurman's case. I'm not going to ask you what he says."

"It's just as well."

"So, you finessed him out of the doorman's address, interviewed him, and came up empty."

"I didn't come up empty."

"Did you come up full?"

"Alice."

"Well, what did you get?"

"The guy was nervous about his relationship with the super."

"You think the doorman and the super killed her?"

"Don't be silly."

"Then I don't understand."

"I got the feeling he and the doorman had something going on. Something illicit. Like running call girls or peddling cocaine."

"Typical."

"What do you mean?"

"Your mind immediately goes to sex and drugs. It's a wonder you missed rock and roll."

"Didn't seem logical."

"Sex and drugs does? I hope Richard isn't depending on you to save him."

"What are you blaming me for not doing?"

"Did I say I was blaming you?"

"You don't have to. I can always tell."

"How?"

"For one thing, it's your default position. In this case there were subtle clues. A tip of the head. A slope of a breast."

"You infer blame from the slope of my breast."

"Why not? You always do."

"Let's not be juvenile. What is it you think I'm trying to tell you?"

"Usually it's something I missed. Though, in this case there's nothing *to* miss."

"Are you sure about that?"

"All right. What did I miss?"

"I wasn't there."

I took a breath. "Okay. I apologize for whatever slight I may have given you by whatever I did or didn't do. I'm not going to try to figure out what that was. I'm sure you'll tell me in your own good time. I'm a little upset because Richard's life is on the line. So if you want to chalk this one up as a victory, I concede defeat. Just tell me what the hell you're getting at."

Alice was unruffled. "I was just pointing out that if you hadn't gone off on your predictable tangent about sex and drugs, what could you have inferred from the doorman's reluctance to talk about the super?"

"They're gay?"

"Oh, for god's sake."

"Alice, I have no idea what you're getting at. What are you getting at?"

Alice explained as if to a small child. "You're really halfway there. The doorman's reluctant to talk about the super being in the lobby when he locked the door and left, right? When was that?"

"Midnight."

"Says who?"

I opened my mouth. Closed it again. Looked at Alice. "He's lying about the time?"

Alice shrugged. "He's lying about something. Richard says he was out at eleven fifteen. The driver says he was out at eleven forty-five. The doorman says he was out at eleven forty-five. What does that tell you?"

It might have told me more had Alice not leaned over when she said that. The neck of my pocket t-shirt was old and stretched by years of washing. It gaped. To a middle-aged married man, such pleasures are few and far between. I found myself distracted. "Um . . ." I ventured.

Alice was getting tired of the Socratic method, which I'm sure worked much better for Socrates without cleavage. "Come on, Stanley. This isn't that hard."

"You've gotta be kidding."

"I'm not. What can you tell from that?"

"You can tell a lot of things. That doesn't make 'em true."

"I disagree. You can draw a lot on inferences. But there's one thing you absolutely know."

"Alice, I'm not in the mood. Just tell me what."

"Both times can't be right."

"Huh?"

"Richard says eleven fifteen, the other two say a quarter to twelve. Someone is wrong."

"Most likely Richard."

"Why, because it's two against one?"

"For one thing. He's also got a horse in the race. He's an interested party. He'd have a reason to lie."

"And the other two wouldn't?"

"No. Why would they?"

"I have no idea. But that's no reason to categorically reject it. That doesn't mean it isn't possible."

"No, but it isn't probable. Come on, we're talking rational here. What logically could have happened. We're not building a hypothetical. We're not saying, yes, it could have happened even though it's an astronomical long shot."

"What's an astronomical long shot?"

"That two men could have independently picked the exact same wrong time, a half hour different than the correct time it actually happened."

Alice nodded. "Yes, that defies the laws of probability."

"So?"

"So what if they didn't?"

My head was coming off. "I beg your pardon?"

"What if they didn't independently pick it?"

"You mean they were in on it and conspired to frame Richard?"

"Of course not. I mean, it could have happened, but it's a hell of a long shot too. No, I mean what if they didn't independently pick the time?"

"Then they conspired together. You can't have it both ways, Alice."

"You're missing the point."

"If they didn't conspire together, how did they pick the same time?"

"Easy."

It was easier with the car service. Richard was the customer. He hired them, he paid them, they would want to give him service.

At least that was the theory. In practice the desk was manned by a sour-looking dispatcher with suspicious eyes. She'd already been questioned by the police, and what the hell was I doing back?

I was quick to assure her I was not the police, I was the representative of her valued customer. If that warmed her heart, she hid it well.

"Can't talk to you," she said.

"Why not?"

"It's a police investigation."

"Exactly."

"And you're not the police."

"I'm the representative of Richard Rosenberg."

"He's not with the police either."

"No, he's not. But he's your customer, I'm his representative, and he wants me to ask you some questions."

"He's got no right to do that."

"Actually, he does. He's a customer, and he's entitled to review the bill. He hired your car service last night, and he wants to know what he's being charged for it."

"That was prenegotiated."

"I'm sure it was. That doesn't alter the situation."

"Yes, it does. He's being charged exactly what he agreed to pay."

"That's all well and good, but I can't take your word for it."

"Well, you're going to have to."

"No, I'm not. If you can't understand why, Mr. Rosenberg is a lawyer and I'm sure he'll be able to explain it to you. It'll be better if you don't make him do it in court, because that will mean that he's suing the company and will probably name you as a codefendant."

She blinked.

"Which is totally ridiculous," I said. "Unless, of course, the police instructed you not to cooperate with Mr. Rosenberg. If the police specifically asked you to withhold information you have from Mr. Rosenberg, that is a perfectly defensible claim, and you're completely off the hook. It might get a cop or two suspended, but I'm sure they won't hold it against you."

That should have done the trick. I wasn't asking for anything to which I wasn't entitled, and there was no reason the woman shouldn't show it to me.

Apparently logic was not her strong suit. I'm not sure what was—most likely not charm and grace, but logic was definitely off the table. The woman set her lips in a firm line and glared at me.

I whipped out my cell phone, called Rosenberg and Stone.

Wendy or Janet answered. Richard employs two switchboard girls who happen to have identical voices. "Rosenberg and Stone," said Wendy or Janet.

"It's Stanley," I said, my standard greeting, since I never know who to say hello to.

"Stanley. Glad you called. I was just about to beep you. I've got a case."

"Yeah," I said. "I need you to type a summons."

"Huh?"

"Hang on, I'll get you the information."

"What in the world are you talking about?"

"What, you have to get a form? Go ahead, I'll hold."

Wendy/Janet was baffled. "Stanley, didn't you hear me? I have to give you the name of the client."

"Yeah, I'll give you the name."

"No, I have to give *you* the name."

"Right. Hang on, I'll get you the name." I covered the phone, said to the dispatcher, "I'm going to need your name."

The woman was baffled. "What do you think you're doing?"

"I'm hauling you into court. So I can get the information." I pointed at her plastic name tag. "Your name is Rose. Wanna give me your last name? Or should I add that to the list of charges?"

"Charges?"

"Yeah. They're adding up. At the moment we have conspiracy to defraud, theft, accessory before and after the fact of a felony. Most of those you should be able to beat. Unless Richard's been overcharged. He hates to be overcharged. I think he gets more pleasure out of the criminal conviction than the money he makes in the civil case. So if you cooperate in filling out the summons, it'll probably go better for you. If we have to get it through independent investigation, Richard is apt to be annoyed."

She showed me the report. Richard had been charged for an hour of overtime.

9

Joey Dodge fancied himself quite the lady's man. Maybe he was, in a cheap, obvious way, with greasy hair, flashy dress, men's cologne, an image that fought hard to say masculine and not gay. I wasn't sure he was winning the battle.

Joey lived in a bachelor pad on the Upper East Side, a one-room walk-up bachelor pad but an East Side address nonetheless. Which is probably what he kept it for. I couldn't imagine him bringing a woman there. I'm sure he always talked his way into her apartment, when and if that ever happened.

Are you getting the impression I don't like the guy? Good guess. And I didn't just begrudge him his youth. I begrudged him his cocky assurance, born of a lack of inhibiting intelligence that might embarrass a smarter person into feeling self-conscious about the macho, arrogant stupidity with which he was making a horse's ass of himself. Oh, to be single, young, and stupid.

"So," I said, "you're the guy who actually drove them around?" I figured buttering the guy up couldn't hurt.

I figured right.

He nodded enthusiastically. "Pretty amazing, huh? Gorgeous thing like that. Hard to believe she's dead."

"You recognized her on the news?"

"How could I miss her? I'll remember that girl forever."

"You called the police?"

"I called the car service. Told 'em that was the girl I drove."

"What did they tell you to do?"

"Are you kidding me? Cooperate with the police. Company doesn't want any trouble, and it certainly wasn't our fault."

"So, what'd you tell 'em?"

"Told 'em what I did. Picked up the guy, picked up the girl, drove 'em to dinner, drove 'em home."

"You waited while they had dinner?"

"That was the job."

"Kind of boring."

"I had the game on. It went quick."

"And after dinner?"

"I drove her home and they went in."

"Did you know the guy?"

"Sure. Richard Rosenberg. Drove him before."

"What about the girl?"

"Sure. Drove 'em both." He shook his head. "How the hell does a guy like him get a girl like that?" He preened slightly, as if showing me the type of guy who ought to get a girl like that.

"And you waited while he was inside?"

"Yeah."

"How long was that?"

"Long enough."

He said it with a knowing leer. Whether he meant long enough for sex or murder I'm not sure.

"Police satisfied with that answer?"

"No. They wanted to know when."

"What'd you tell 'em?"

"He was out of there at a quarter to twelve."

"How you so sure of the time?"

"That's my job."

"Uh huh. You get paid by the job or the hour?"

"I get paid by the job *and* by the hour."

"What's that mean?"

"The job's a flat rate. If it runs long I get more."

"And this job did?"

"It did, as a matter of fact."

"Is that unusual?"

"No. Guy's out with a girl, it often runs long. Guy wants it to, you know what I mean?"

"Yeah. So, in this case. Wanna walk me through the time frame?"

"How you mean?"

"You get paid for the job. How long is that?"

"Six hours."

"Starting when?"

He looked at me like why was I asking, but he wasn't sure if he could tell me to go to hell.

"Okay. I pick him up at six o'clock. That's when the time starts. Not when I leave my apartment, when I pick the guy up. Which is hardly fair. I mean, yeah, this was only fifteen minutes, but what if he lived in East Oshkosh? We drove uptown, picked up the girl, drove 'em to a fancy steakhouse in Brooklyn. After dinner I drove them back to her apartment, waited for him to come out, drove him home. Dropped him off at twelve twenty. That's why there's overtime. A guy's got a five-, ten-minute grace period, but anything over fifteen he's gotta pay."

"A whole hour?"

"We don't do half hours."

"So he came out of the building at a quarter to twelve?"

"That's right."

"What was he like?"

"What do you mean?"

"Was he nervous? Agitated? The way he'd be if he just killed someone."

"He was panting. But I didn't think it was because he killed someone, if you know what I mean."

I did. "So you saw her on TV, you called the agency, they told you to call the police?"

"That's right."

"Which you did?"

"Yeah."

"Right away?"

"Damn straight, right away. You think I want to get into trouble?"

"And you told them about Richard Rosenberg going in and coming out at a quarter to twelve?"

"Of course."

10

Richard wasn't pleased. "Wendy said you blew her off."

"I didn't blow her off, Richard. She missed a signal."

"You gave Wendy a signal?"

"She didn't have to pick up on it. All she had to do was not scream into the phone."

"Did she scream into the phone?"

"No."

"So what are you griping about?"

"You said I blew her off."

"Well, you did, didn't you? You may have had a reason, but it's not like you didn't do it."

"Richard, are you being incredibly annoying because your mind can't handle the enormity of the situation?"

"Got me," Richard said. "That's exactly what I was doing. Now that you've seen through me, I'll give up that shallow façade, go home, and slit my wrists."

"Richard—"

"Stanley, I don't know how to break it to you, but I didn't do it. And I'm too damn good a lawyer to take the fall, even for a crime I didn't commit. I've got you looking into it because I'd like to know, but I'm not particularly worried. I asked the girls to put you back on the clock because investigating this shouldn't be a full-time job. It's not that important."

"You want me back on the clock?"

"Don't you need the work?"

"I do. I thought you wanted me to do this."

"In your spare time. It's not a career. Anyway, that's my assessment. Unless your investigation has turned up anything. If people are trying to frame me, that's another matter altogether. So, is anyone trying to frame me?"

"Well—"

"Well? What do you mean, well? Either they are or they aren't."

"The driver of the car may have screwed with the time element."

"I know he screwed with the time element. The guy got it wrong. I was out at eleven fifteen. The cops think it was a quarter to twelve. That's a huge difference, considering the time of death."

"Time of death?"

"Yeah, the medical examiner puts the time of death between eleven and one."

"How'd you get that?"

"You think you're the only one with connections? A woman down at the morgue likes me. I got her fifty thousand bucks for a thumb she slammed in a car door."

I was sure he had. The mind boggled.

"So, you think the driver screwed with the time to frame me?"

"No, I think he just did. Framing you is coincidental."

"How could it be coincidental if the doorman says so too?"

"The driver pads his paycheck by inflating his hours to get overtime. He clocked out at twelve twenty, the time he says he dropped you off at your apartment. That's already in the books. The guy had turned it in. So he was stuck with it. When the cops asked him when you came out, he realized eleven fifteen would mean it took him over an hour to drive you home. So he fudged the time."

"But how'd he get the doorman to back him up?"

"He didn't have to. The doorman goes off duty at midnight. He locks the front door and goes home. From midnight until eight in the morning, the front door's locked and the super lets people in."

"So what?"

"Did you see the doorman when you went out?"

"How the hell should I know?"

"Because you're on the hook for murder."

Richard's head snapped up. He looked at me sharply.

"Sorry. Isn't that the type of thing you say to your clients? Not that you defend a lot of murderers, but aren't you always hitting them with some short, snappy, don't-be-a-jerk type of statement?"

"Are you implying I'm a jerk?"

"Don't be silly. But it's a murder case, so it matters. Let me help you out. I'm willing to bet when you came out at eleven fifteen the doorman was busy chatting with someone at the desk."

Richard nodded. "Now that you mention it, I think there was a food delivery of some sort. I remember thinking it was kind of late for takeout."

"That's why he didn't see you at eleven fifteen, and he's so quick to say he saw you at eleven forty-five."

"Why?"

"Because he wasn't there. He'd already gone home."

"How do you figure?"

"The super doesn't come out and sit on the desk all night. He's in his apartment, only comes out when someone buzzes the door.

42

He doesn't come out when the doorman goes off, so the doorman doesn't wait for him. He just locks the front door and goes home. He's eager to get out of there, so he goes home early. You can bet your bottom dollar, last night he left between eleven thirty and a quarter to twelve."

"Don't people notice he's not there?"

"Sure, but he locks the front door when he goes to the bathroom too. When that happens, people use their keys. It's only visitors have to buzz the door. And how many visitors are there between eleven thirty and midnight? As you say, the eleven fifteen delivery was unusual.

"So, at a quarter of twelve the guy's gone. How does he pick that as the time you left? He didn't. The cops did. They let him pick it the same way a magician forces a card. 'Pick a time, any time, don't show me the time, put it back in the deck.' They let it drop, 'The driver says you came out at a quarter to twelve,' doorman jumps on it like a lifeline."

"I see," Richard said. "That's just a theory?"

"You want me to nail it down? Stake out the place, get evidence of the doorman leaving early?"

"Hell, no. You'll just tip him off. If you haven't already. Bad enough you asked him all these questions, put him on his guard."

Well, that was depressing. I'd been looking forward to telling Alice how well her theory had panned out. Now I'd have to downplay Richard's assessment of the result.

"Is there anything you *do* want me doing?"

"Oh, sure," Richard said. He tipped back in his desk chair, cocked his head. "I believe Wendy has a case for you."

11

I signed up Barry White of Jersey City, New Jersey. It wasn't easy. It was all I could do to stop myself from saying, "We got it together now, didn't we, babe?" Seeing as how the man was in a certain degree of pain, that wouldn't have been appropriate. Aside from that, it would have been appropriate since the surgeons had gotten it together and stitched it up and held it there with a metal pin in order to keep the top half of his fibula from detaching from the bottom half of his fibula, which undoubtedly would have caused him more pain than he was currently feeling.

Mr. White had tripped on a pothole in the street and wanted to sue Jersey City for umpty million dollars. I figured the claim might have had more validity had the gentleman not fallen at two in the morning on his way home from the Bucket of Suds, where he had been drinking steadily since four in the afternoon, but I'm not the lawyer. I just sign 'em up. Richard decides whether to take them. I'd have given odds he'd dump this one, but then Richard was still suing the City of New York on behalf of a man who jumped in front of a subway train. The only bone of contention keeping the suit alive was just how much the city was willing to pony up.

I took Mr. White's story down word for word. If called upon to testify, I would tell the absolute truth. Which wasn't likely. In all the time I'd been working for Richard, I had almost never been called upon to testify.

Wendy/Janet beeped me on my way back over the George Washington Bridge. That was too bad. I had a cell phone, but I don't use it while driving, not wanting to become one of those people who have accidents while doing so, several of whom I've actually signed up as Richard's clients. The switchboard girls don't have my cell phone number and still beep me with a pager. When that happens I stop the car and call in.

Hard to do in the middle of the George Washington Bridge. Instead of taking the West Side Highway downtown, I got off on Riverside Drive, pulled over, and called the office.

"Rosenberg and Stone," said Wendy/Janet.

"You beeped me."

"Oh. Stanley. Glad you called."

She always says that, even though she beeped me. At least one of them always says that. I have no idea which it might be.

"Got another case?"

"No. You want one?"

It was like swimming through molasses. "Why did you beep me?"

"Oh. Richard wants you to see the judge."

12

"I'm seeing you as a courtesy to Mr. Rosenberg," Judge Peters said. "He called, offered his condolences, asked if you could stop by. Apparently there are some things he wanted to know but felt awkward asking under the circumstances. I'm not sure why. Richard Rosenberg and I are not likely to ever have a case where I would have to recuse myself."

"So there's no reason you can't talk to me."

"None. I doubt it will help."

"Why is that?"

"I don't know anything about it."

"Well, you knew the woman. She worked for you."

"Yes. But I don't know anything about her personal life."

"Did you know she was seeing Richard Rosenberg?"

"I'd heard a rumor to that effect."

"Had you discussed it with her?"

He looked at me sharply. "What's that got to do with anything?"

"Just curious. I never met the woman. I'm trying to get a feel for her. If you had any conversation regarding Richard Rosenberg, it might be illuminating."

"I assure you it wouldn't."

"What was the nature of the conversation?"

"I never said I had a conversation."

"Right. And you're a judge, and you're smart enough to know what I'm getting at. If, for instance, you advised her *against* going out with Mr. Rosenberg, it would be interesting."

"Why?"

"Because she continued to do so. Which would earn your displeasure unless she took pains to see you didn't know about it. Which, I assume, would require nothing more than not mentioning it."

Judge Peters took a breath. "I may have made a remark about negligence lawyers in general. They are outside of the scope of my experience. I shouldn't generalize, but what contact I have had has not been pleasant. I have even been the victim of frivolous lawsuits. Prominent men often are." He grimaced. "I'm sorry. That was arrogant, but you know what I mean. Judges, doctors, professional men are often sued. Some men will pay to make it go away. I, as you might assume, will not."

"So, you don't know Mr. Rosenberg personally, except he is one of the scum-sucking bottom-feeders you sometimes have to deal with."

"Now, see here—"

I put up my hand. "Please. He would be the first to agree. The man has made a small fortune. If anyone were the likely target of a frivolous lawsuit it would be Richard. The only deterrent is the fact it wouldn't cost him anything because he would be able to represent himself, and he doesn't lose. But that's neither here nor there. The point is, warning her that he is a negligence lawyer is perfectly natural and the right and proper thing to do. Aside from that, did you know anything about the woman's personal life?"

"I did not. I only knew about Mr. Rosenberg because one of the other clerks was discussing it."

"And what was her job? What did she do?"

"The same as the other law clerks. Look up files. Keep the paperwork straight."

"Would she be present at depositions?"

"What do you know about depositions?"

"Just the fact they have them."

"Lawyers do. I'm a judge."

"You don't take depositions?"

"I hear them read in court."

I nodded. "With regard to the case you're handling. How was she involved in that?"

"Her death has nothing to do with the case."

"How can you be sure?"

"She's a clerk. She doesn't know anything, she's no danger to anyone."

"Well, not now. If she wasn't a clerk, she might be a danger to someone?"

"I didn't say that."

"You implied it. She's not a danger because she's a clerk. What is the case you're working on?"

"I'm not working on it. I'm presiding."

"Sorry."

"No big deal. You just spoke of it as if I were an ADA. If you're as confused as you say you are, I should set your straight."

"Believe me, it's not an act. I was born confused. So can you tell me generally about the case? It has something to do with the Bank of New York?"

"No, Global Banking."

"What's that?"

"Another bank. It's not the Bank of New York, but it would like to be."

"And what's the issue?"

"Do you really want to know? Illegal spending, trading, insider mortgages, illegally structured interest rates, false advertising. Get the picture?"

"Manipulating money?"

"That's a good catchall."

"And who are the defendants?"

"Global Banking."

"Who are the *people*?"

"The owner, the president, the CEO. Larry Longmore, Chester Adams, Hank Greengrass."

"And did Jeannie know any of them?"

"She knew who they were. She was in court enough."

"Did she ever speak to any of them?"

"Not to my knowledge."

"Well, let me put it this way. If I were a defendant in this action, what sort of edge might I get by befriending a clerk of the court?"

"Absolutely none. The clerk of the court has no influence over the proceedings."

"How about inside information?"

"What information? She didn't know anything, and it wouldn't have helped. If you think her murder has something to do with the case, you're on the wrong track."

"What's the right track?"

"That's a figure of speech. I have no idea. I hope Mr. Rosenberg is innocent. Frankly, I know nothing about it."

"And before Mr. Rosenberg?"

"What?"

"Who did she go out with?"

"I wouldn't know."

"You wouldn't have heard from one of the other clerks?"

"I don't listen to gossip."

"Unless it involves a negligence lawyer."

"Low blow. But accurate. You're rather astute for someone without a legal education," he said drily. "At least I'm assuming you have no legal education."

"I was going to, but I heard you had to go to school."

"That's usually required." He shrugged. "Though, considering some lawyers I know . . ."

"Mind if I talk to your law clerks?"

"As long as you don't interfere with their work."

"When would I be able to do that?"

"Tomorrow, when court breaks for lunch."

"What time is that?"

"When I get hungry."

13

They looked like the guiltiest scumbags ever to come down the pike. One was older, with white hair, a crooked nose, and a beatific smile, kind of like the cat who swallowed the money and wasn't about to give it back. The other two were cut from the same mold, that is to say, a large pile of mold from which an artist had sculpted two villains. One was thin and wiry. The other wasn't.

Representing the three defendants were no less than six lawyers, each older and more conservatively dressed than the last. I couldn't tell what their individual functions were, but they all seemed to be competing in a constipation contest, in which case the one to the right of the younger sleazeball was winning.

Do I sound prejudiced? I'd have like to have been called as a juror for that case. The chances of my being taken would have been nil.

Opposing the attorneys were two ADAs, young, aggressive, also conservatively dressed, though not as ostentatiously so, just two practical, no-nonsense men cutting through the bullshit and getting to the facts of the case.

Or at least trying to. For every question asked by an ADA there were at least three objections, some of which I'd heard before but others probably never uttered in a court of law. It would have been interesting to hear them argued, but such discussions took place at the sidebar out of earshot of the jury. All I got to hear was, "Sustained" or "Overruled." If you're keeping score, *overruled* was winning, but as it took only one *sustained* to trump two *overruled*, not a lot of questions were getting answered.

The jurors looked numb. I wondered how many days of this they'd had to endure.

Scuttling back and forth to the judge's bench was a neatly dressed young man, whom I took to be a law clerk, carrying papers and law books. Once he carried a glass of water, which Judge Peters accepted with far more enthusiasm than anything else.

Finally the judge had had enough. Banging the gavel, he declared, "Court is in recess until two o'clock."

I corralled the presumed law clerk, a young man with horn-rimmed glasses and a somewhat nerdy look.

"You clerk for Judge Peters?"

He looked at me as if I were a fool not to know. "Yeah?"

"I'm investigating the murder of your colleague and I need to ask you a few questions."

He seemed startled. "What in the world for? I know nothing about it."

"You knew her. You worked with her. Your impressions would be valuable. I realize you don't know anything about the crime; I'm interested in finding out something about the person."

"I'm not sure I should talk to you."

"I've already talked to the judge. He's the one who suggested I come to court and ask you."

"He didn't say anything to me."

"It's not his place to ask you to cooperate with me. But if you want to ask him if he minds if you do, that's quite all right."

"I'm on my way to lunch."

"Fine. I'm buyin'. Invite the other clerks."

"There's just two of us now Jeannie's gone."

He seemed slightly aggrieved, probably resented the extra work.

The other law clerk turned out to be a woman, a slender young thing with a particularly drab appearance. The death of Jeannie Atkins had left her the most attractive girl clerk, a distinction she would undoubtedly hold until the judge hired another.

We crowded into a greasy spoon near the courthouse and ordered a round of cheeseburgers.

"So, what can you tell me about Jeannie?" I said.

"We don't know anything about Jeannie," the nerdy clerk said. His name might have been Alex, but I couldn't swear to it.

"You knew she was seeing Richard Rosenberg."

"That was hardly a secret," the girl said. I was even less sure of her name.

He grinned. I refined nerdy to dorky. "Not after you spread it around."

"Hey," she protested. "*You* told *me*."

"So, what *was* a secret?" I said.

She frowned. "What?"

"Well, you say everyone knew about Richard Rosenberg. Was there anything everyone *didn't* know about?"

"How would we know if we didn't know?" Dorky Clerk said. He might have meant it as a joke but managed to make it sound petulant.

"Well, one of you might have known something she wasn't spreading around."

"Yeah, well, *I* didn't," Plain Jane said. "God knows what she might have told him."

"She share secrets with you?"

He gawked. "Me? Nah. We weren't close."

"Who was?"

They looked at each other.

Our burgers arrived, a welcome interruption. After a sorting of plates and passing of condiments, we all dug in.

After a bite or two I posed the question again. "So who was close to Jeannie?"

He shrugged. "None of us were, really."

"So who'd she tell she was seeing Richard Rosenberg?"

"It wasn't me."

"Me either," the girl said.

"We're talking immaculate conception?" I said.

"I heard one of the ADAs talking," Dorky Clerk said. "I think he was trying to date her. He sounded miffed."

"What ADA was that?"

The girl put up her hands. "You don't want to get anyone in trouble."

"Trouble?" I said. "Why would he get in trouble? He didn't do anything, did he?"

"Of course not," she said.

"So who are we talking about?"

"Stu Edelstein," Dorky Clerk blurted.

Plain Jane shot him a dirty look.

"Who's Stu Edelstein?"

"An ADA."

"On this case?"

"Yeah."

"One of the two in court today?"

"The younger one," Plain Jane said.

"Of course," I said. The older one was younger than me. "He asked her out?"

"I'm not sure what he asked her," Dorky Clerk said, "but he wasn't happy with the answer."

"So he was pissed off when he heard she was dating a negligence lawyer?"

"It wasn't so much it was a negligence lawyer as it wasn't him."

"Anyone else show any interest in Jeannie?"

Plain Jane shrugged. "Wouldn't know."

"So, a guy interested in her was working on the case. What's the case?"

"Why?" Dorky Clerk said.

"Just wondering what she might have done that got her killed."

"I should think that was obvious," Plain Jane said. It must have been fun to be catty with no competition.

"Yeah," I said, "and if you're right, the police shouldn't have a hard time. But if you're wrong, then we gotta look for something else. I'm going on the assumption that you're wrong. Which is no reflection on you. Simply as a premise because the opposite doesn't help me."

"You're working for Richard Rosenberg?" Dorky Clerk said.

"Would that be a problem?"

"You said the judge knows you're talking to us."

"He does, and he's not going to hold anything you say against you. Unless you say Rosenberg couldn't have done it because Judge Peters did."

"As if," Plain Jane said.

"Why do you say that?"

"No reason."

"Yeah, there was, and now you're uptight about it. I'm not a threat to you. Nothing you say will be used against you in a court of law. Or be reported to the judge. If there's a reason you said that, I'd like to know."

"She thinks he's gay," Dorky Clerk said.

"Hey!" Plain Jane protested. "I never said that."

"Which is so stupid. Just because he's not into you doesn't mean he's gay."

"No, just because he's into *you* means he is."

"He's not into me."

"How could he *not* be? You've got your nose buried in his ass."

"So," I said, trying to steer the conversation back to something halfway useful. "What is it about this case that could have gotten someone killed?"

"How about the fact there's millions of dollars involved?" Dorky Clerk said.

"Is that right?" I said. "Are you talking fines or future revenues lost or are you talking giving back?"

"Whoa!" he said. "Giving something back? Not even an option. You can find these guys guilty of everything from rape to arson, but nobody's giving any money back. The bank stole it fair and square. Fines and penalties, yes, but giving money back? It's against their religion."

"How about going to jail?"

"Rather not," Dorky Clerk said. I was surprised to find he had a sense of humor.

"Seriously," I said. "Is that an option?"

He shook his head. "Not a chance."

"Why not?"

"The trial would have to end first."

14

ADA Edelstein had a chip on his shoulder. And it wasn't just frustrations with the objections of the defense. He could have had a fight with the wife, he could have felt his career wasn't taking off the way it should, or he could have murdered a cock tease of a law clerk who blew him off for an older, shorter, and undoubtedly richer attorney from the Dark Side, the type for whom *shyster* was too good a name.

Yeah, I was back in court after lunch. Considering what I got out of the law clerks, the guy was my only lead. Actually, him or his case. It could be personal or it could be business. Amazing how everything comes back to *The Godfather.*

If it was his case I was out of luck. Because the amount I could understand, even without the legal objections, was nil, and what with sidebars coming left and right, not to mention having missed countless weeks of this sucker, I'd have had more luck explaining quantum physics to a class of hyperactive kindergarteners.

So I watched him for his own sake, and he certainly was a sour individual. I would not have wanted to be cross-examined by him, all saving technical objections notwithstanding.

His disdain was so pervasive, it was a while before I realized it had a focus. That focus was none other than the judge. ADA Edelstein managed to give the impression the judge was biased against him, that what would appear to be simple legal rulings were actually part of a diabolical persecution carried out by a person in power for no other reason than that he could.

After a while I refined that theory. The vindictive campaign was not arbitrary but specific. The tormenter had personal motivation.

By the time I'd figured that out, other dynamics had begun to evolve. Of the other attorneys, there was one whose dislike of Edelstein rivaled his dislike of the judge.

The embittered attorney was the only female in the group, one of the two attorneys who appeared to be representing Crooknose, the older defendant with the white hair. I couldn't tell if gender played a role in her disdain, but I would not have been surprised to find ADA Edelstein had dated her at one time or another. The attorney was easy on the eyes, with far more breasts than I would have expected on a lawyer, despite the law shows on TV. The shows are fiction. The women on them have been chosen for their physical attributes, no years of law school required. That's not to say attractive lawyers don't exist in real life, that's just to say it's not the first thing I think of. And attractive women *are* pretty much the first thing I think of.

Anyway, the busty if conservatively dressed defense attorney was favoring ADA Edelstein with the type of frozen smile a young woman usually reserves for the young man who has dumped her for another woman. I wondered if the other woman was Jeannie.

At any rate, the current bone of contention in the Global Banking case was the Washburn memo. It had been introduced into evidence over the objections of every lawyer within a twenty-five-mile radius of the courthouse, and it was being dissected so thoroughly that even I was beginning to understand. Apparently the memo had been circulated long before the start of any courtroom proceedings or even before any had been contemplated, at least by the district attorney's office.

The proceeding had been anticipated, however, by Global Bank. The Washburn memo basically consisted of instructions on how to thwart such proceedings, should they ever occur. It was as close to a smoking gun as such things come, sort of like saying, "If the cops come around flush the evidence down the toilet." It enjoined all employees of Global Bank to deny any knowledge of a particular offshore account. Which was the basis for another pitched battle that seemed certain to send the proceedings into yet another week.

"And what did you take that to mean?" ADA Edelstein asked.

His female counterpart led the barrage of objections. As the small army retired to the sidebar, I watched the ensuing tableau and tried to observe the dynamics. You have to understand I couldn't hear a word. But from facial expressions, body language—because a good eight people were crowded around the judge—I formed the following impressions.

The judge was aware that the attractive attorney was attractive. ADA Edelstein was aware that the judge was aware that the attractive attorney was attractive. The attractive attorney was aware that she was attractive and aware both men knew it.

And whether it was merely a coincidence, hers was the objection that was sustained.

None of this offered me any insight whatsoever into the workings of Global Bank.

15

I staked out the courthouse.

Actually I waited on the street to see who came out, but staking out the courthouse sounds much more official.

It didn't take that long. Apparently it's not like a basketball game, where the teams have to go back to the dressing room and shower and put on street clothes. They just say good-bye and walk out. I suppose a lawyer wants to talk to a client now and then, but after four weeks of this shit what is there to say? "I thought our objections are holding up pretty well—you like the way I improvised the outside-the-realm-of-logical supposition? It didn't get sustained, but did you see the look on that ADA's face?" No, they pretty much hung it up and went home. I was lucky to beat 'em out to the street.

For the most part. Some lawyers were faster than others. I recognized several defense lawyers, but of course I had more to choose from. The two with the thin and wiry sleazeball came out, happy as clams, visions of billable hours dancing in their heads. The two lawyers with the fatter sleazeball came next. They didn't look quite as happy. I figured trouble at home, since nothing about the case could be bothering them. Unless they had a mortgage with Global Bank.

I was beginning to wonder if there was a separate door for ADAs when the older of the two came out. He looked happy enough, considering he wasn't getting paid by Global Bank. Unless he was, which would be a whole new angle in itself, would lead to an even more explosive court case. Though how a case could be less explosive than the one I'd been snoring through would be hard to imagine.

Next up was another attorney. I almost missed him because he came out alone. The poor man didn't really have his own personality. In my mind, he existed only as the attorney paired with the attractive young attorney. Take her away, and there was no reason to notice him.

So where was she? Not that it mattered, of course, but I was grasping at straws, and she was one I'd like to grasp. And where was the other ADA, for that matter? Could they be together?

They could not. No sooner did I have that thought than young ADA Edelstein came bopping out the door and headed for Chambers Street.

I was tempted to tail him. The only thing holding me back was then I would lose the girl. Well, not that that was the only thing holding me back. That it was a totally fruitless endeavor might have had something to do with it. Anyway, I wanted to see the scenario play out. And the only two actors left were the girl and the judge.

Wrong again. The three defendants came out together, talking and laughing and lighting cigars. Cigars, for Christ's sake. I mean they didn't just win the Kentucky Derby, they survived another day in court. But there they were, "Hey, not one of us went to jail yet, light 'em up!" Their lack of concern should have been enough to convince me they didn't kill a law clerk, but then men with that much power and disdain for practically everything could probably whack off a few heads over lunch break and appear not the least bit ruffled when court reconvened. But for my money they were innocent, which, I realized, was a hell of an admission, seeing as how I was rooting for anyone but Richard.

ADA Edelstein came out next. Alone. That was disappointing. If he'd just come out with the girl. I'd already fantasized wild conspiracy theories, with the two of them having hot sex and plotting to throw the case and having to silence Jeannie the law clerk when she got wind of it. But, no, there he was, leaving the building, a little late, probably just had to call his wife and pick up a quart of milk on the way home.

But where was *she*? And where was the judge? And was there something to the judge's assessment of her technical objections? Could they be holed up in his chambers having a quickie after court?

Or was there a separate entrance for judges? If he was sneaking in a side door, it would be harder to yell, "Here comes the judge!" On the other hand, if he was banging the law clerk, you could yell, "Here comes the judge!"

It occurred to me I'd been on stakeout way too long.

And there she was, out the front door, cool as ice, fresh, clean, looking like a million bucks. Or at least looking a hell of a lot better than anything else in that courtroom.

She was, as befitted an attorney, discreetly dressed. Her hair was pinned up, her makeup, if any, was understated. Her conservatively cut blouse was filled out in a most unlawyerly way, and her brief-case swung next to a derriere that might have launched, if not a thousand ships, at least in the high eight hundreds.

I decided to follow her. Don't give me any credit for it. Half the PIs in New York would have followed her.

She walked down to the subway station at Chambers Street. That's what I figured. It was the Lexington Avenue line, and she struck me as an East Side girl.

She might have been, but she didn't take the subway. She went into a coffee shop on Chambers. Not a Starbucks, just a generic shop where the coffee was equally expensive. I didn't follow her in. Richard would gag at a five-dollar latte on my expense account. I would be lucky to escape unflayed.

I stood on the sidewalk and watched through the window.

She didn't buy a coffee. She pulled up a chair at a table in the back opposite ADA Edelstein.

It's great when your theories pan out. All right, ADA Edelstein's having an affair with the attractive attorney was more of a guess than a theory. Nor did it mean Richard's law clerk had found out they were having a tryst so they had to kill her. And why such a revelation should be worth murder was beyond me. I certainly hoped that wasn't it, because I had just been promoted to the position of the person who could make that revelation and would need to be eliminated.

Well, now I could justify buying that expensive cup of coffee. This was one conversation I had to get close enough to hear.

They got up and headed for the door, just as I was starting in. I felt a moment of total panic before I realized they didn't know me. They had no idea who I was. As far as they were concerned, I was just some poor schmuck willing to blow a bundle on a cup of joe.

I held the door for 'em, let 'em go out. Of course, then I had to go in. I thought about snapping my fingers, pretending I remembered something, the type of shit you do before you realize no one cares, no one's paying the least bit of attention to you. You could get an Academy Award for your I-have-to-pick-up-my-pants-before-the-tailor-closes act, and no one in the world is going to give a damn about your motivation. So I didn't whack myself on the forehead and cry, "Oh, damn it!" or any other utterly inappropriate thing. I just went in the door, turned around, and watched them through the window.

They walked down the street together, conversing freely. Not freely enough. When I came out of the coffee shop and closed the distance, I couldn't hear a thing. I should have been in front of them. That was out of the question now. I caught up as close as I dared, pretended I was watching the woman's butt. It wasn't that hard to do. But not particularly profitable. Unless you count a slight stirring in my loins.

I was caught flat-footed when Edelstein stepped out in the street and flagged a cab. He held the door, she slid in, he jumped in beside her, and off they went.

It was the only cab within a hundred miles.

18

Richard wasn't pleased.

"You did what?"

"I know you didn't ask me to, but I was concerned."

"You sat in court?"

"Yes."

"For how long?"

"Four hours."

"You expect me to pay for that?"

"Richard—"

"Work I didn't authorize? Work I didn't request?"

"I thought it was important."

"Your *work* is important. Did you do any?"

"No."

"Janet was trying to reach you all afternoon. You didn't answer your beeper."

"You can't wear a beeper in court."

"Oh, there's a reason not to go. Wasn't that a bit of a tipoff?"

"Don't you wanna hear what I got?"

"I know what you got. You got a conspiracy theory about ADAs and law clerks. And judges and defense attorneys. How about the defendants? How do you find them blameless in all this?"

"They were smoking cigars."

"Is that right? Well, I will certainly tell all the clients I defend in the future. Oh, wait a minute. I don't *represent* defendants. I'm a *negligence* lawyer. I represent the *plaintiffs*. Defendants are the ones I demolish. Assuming my ace investigator has his beeper on and brings me the cases."

"I think you're being framed."

"Do you really? Well, then they did a pretty poor job of it. Because there's an hour-and-fifteen-minute window of opportunity after I left where everybody and his brother could have come in and killed her, even with the witnesses fucking up and blowing the time element a half an hour in the prosecution's favor. But, oh no, that's not enough for you, you gotta go out and find some *other* way to demonstrate that I didn't do it. Since no one's saying I did, I can assume the person you're attempting to convince is yourself. Stanley. Relax. The time-space continuum is not crumbling. Good is not bad, up is not down, black is not white. I am no more a killer this week than I was last week. I could no more kill someone than I could sing light opera. And if you put in eight hours tomorrow trying to prove I can't sing opera, don't expect to get paid for it."

"I see your gift for sarcasm is still intact."

"How could it not be? You practically beg for it."

I got up. "I'm sorry I wasted your time. I'll see what Janet wants."

Richard waved me back. "Hang on, hang on. It's too late to start a case today. You can pick it up in the morning."

"Are you sure that's soon enough? With such important clients?"

Richard made a face, shook his head. "No, you don't do sarcasm well. You should take some lessons."

"I can't afford 'em. My boss cherry-picks my hours."

He pointed his finger. "Better. Much better. Sit down, relax. You want a drink?"

"I don't drink."

"Right. I know that." He took out a bottle of some expensive bourbon or other. I'm sure if I'd said yes he'd have managed to slip me rotgut. "All right, so tell me what you learned in court."

"I thought you didn't care."

"I don't. But you did it, so we might as well see what you've got. Aside from gossip and innuendo."

"You don't like the sexy lawyer for the killing?"

"She doesn't live in the building, and it's harder for a woman to get into the building unseen."

"How is that?"

"Are you nuts? Five men and a woman walk into the building, who you gonna notice?"

"Well, when you put it like that."

"No, the law clerk's a better bet."

"Which law clerk?"

"The lady law clerk. Who'd you think?"

"I thought it was harder for a woman to get into the building."

"An attractive woman, yes. You said the law clerk's rather dumpy."

"Are you serious?"

"Of course I am. If it was your theory, you'd be pleased as punch you came up with it."

I thought that over. I wasn't sure it was right, but I was less sure about rejecting it.

"How about the theory the judge also had the hots for Jeannie?"

"And snuck into her apartment and killed her?"

"No, but the lady lawyer wouldn't be pleased that the judge had the hots for her."

"You keep coming back to the lady lawyer."

"She seems like a good bet."

"Because she's banging an ADA. Whoop-de-fuckin'-do. Think she's the first lawyer ever banged an ADA?"

"I bet she's the first lawyer ever banged an ADA who was having an affair with the law clerk you were dating."

"Glib. You do glib well."

"How about the premise?"

"There you get lost. But that's understandable, since no one knows what the hell happened."

"They're not about to, with Sergeant Thurman in charge."

Richard sat bolt upright in his chair. "Sergeant Thurman's in charge?"

"You didn't know that?"

"That's the one detail of the case you managed to leave out."

"He wasn't in charge when you were brought in?"

"How should I know? I wasn't interviewed by a cop. I was taken straight before the ADA."

"Not ADA Edelstein?"

"The one tied up in the Global Bank case? Oh, sure. They gave him the afternoon off so he could interview me."

"Okay, that was stupid."

"My god, Thurman's in charge. I should write my will."

"Which is why I thought the case deserved investigating."

Richard turned his eyes on me. "No, you didn't. You just learned I didn't know Thurman was in charge. As far as you knew, I did and it didn't bother me."

"I can understand your lashing out. It's got to be quite a shock."

"Don't try to be funny. A beautiful woman is dead, I'm on the hook for it, the murder isn't going to be solved, even if the cops come to the obvious conclusion I had nothing to do with it."

"That's certainly my opinion. So, you don't want me to investigate?"

"I want *someone* to investigate. I guess that means you."

"There's a vote of confidence."

"I wondered what the cops were doing. Clearly they're doing nothing."

"You want me to talk to Thurman?"

"Absolutely not! As far as Thurman is concerned, that would just mean I'm guilty."

"So what do you want me to do?"

17

MacAullif wasn't pleased. I think I've said that before. MacAullif was often displeased. And it seemed to correspond with me walking into his office. I wouldn't want to infer cause and effect; still, some of the remarks he'd made would seem to lean in that direction. So did his facial expression, tone of voice, and frequency of expletives. The conclusion that I had not made his day was not hard to come by.

"You want me to talk to Thurman?" MacAullif said. One would have thought I had asked him to gargle horse piss.

"I need to find out about Richard's case."

"Oh, now it's *Richard's* case?"

"It was always Richard's case, MacAullif. If it wasn't, I wouldn't care."

"That's not true, is it? You've pestered me with cases that had nothing to do with anyone."

"I was *hired* to do it."

"You were hired. I don't think anyone specifically hired you to pester me."

"They hired me to help them. Pestering you is a side effect."

"And yet you always make it seem like a perk."

"I'm in a bind, MacAullif. Richard just found out Thurman's in charge."

"He didn't know it?"

"No. Apparently he had other things on his mind."

"I'm sure he did. And you let it slip about Thurman?"

"I didn't realize he didn't know."

"And he flipped out?"

"Wouldn't you? So now he's in a blind panic and wants to know what the hell is going on."

"That's understandable. So why don't you ask Thurman?"

"He told me not to talk to Thurman."

"So why are you bothering me?"

"He didn't tell me not to talk to you."

"Of course not. I have nothing to do with the case."

"Exactly. So you can talk to Thurman for me."

"That's a hollow subterfuge."

"Thurman won't know. He doesn't even know the word *subterfuge*."

"What do you want me to ask him?'"

"Are you kidding? You're a police officer. You don't know what's pertinent information in a murder case?"

"I do. Thurman doesn't." MacAullif picked up a file from his desk, started reading.

"You're not going to talk to Thurman?"

"I can't see any reason I should."

"How about I'm in a bind?"

"I would hate to leave you in a bind."

"So?"

"Life is full of disappointments. I'll have to learn to live with it." MacAullif put down the file. "Stanley, don't be a wuss. You want to know what's on Sergeant Thurman's mind, ask him."

"Richard told me not to."

MacAullif shrugged. "So, do what you always do with me."

"What?"

"Lie."

18

Sergeant Thurman made MacAullif's welcome seem like an embrace. His nose crinkled up, and his face twisted into an expression usually reserved for the beheading of fowl.

"Yes," he said. I figured he was marking time while he thought up some devastating zinger, since words did not generally trip nimbly from his tongue.

"Glad to see you too," I said. "I came to congratulate you on the progress you made on the Atkins case."

That caught him up short. The sarcastic remark he'd been dreaming up obviously did not blend nicely after that. He blinked, snarled, came up with the old standard. "Get the fuck out of my office."

"I would, but the fuck isn't *in* your office."

His head came up. "Huh? None of your lip. I told you, I'm not talking about the case."

"I know. But I am."

"What?"

"I'm not asking you about the case. I'm *telling* you about the case."

"What are you talking about?"

"I've been doing some investigating."

"You've got no right to do that."

"Yeah, but it's done. And I know some things, and I'm here to tell you."

"Why?"

"I have to. I can't withhold evidence in a murder case. I could go to jail."

"You could get the shit pounded out of you."

"That too. Neither of which I'd like. So I want to tell you what I know so I'm off the hook."

"What do you know?"

Victory. Instead of throwing me through the wall, the guy was going to listen. I preferred that.

Of course I had nothing to tell him, but you can't have everything.

"Jeannie Atkins was clerking for Judge Peters on the Global Bank case."

"Think I didn't know that?"

"You know what it's about?"

"Who cares what it's about?"

"Three defendants, six attorneys, two ADAs, a judge, and three law clerks. That's a lot of people, but there's several billion dollars involved. That's why people care."

"So?"

"Jeannie Atkins worked the case. That made her privy to certain information that was important to someone."

"Who?"

"Someone who didn't want it known."

"Bullshit."

"Why do you say that?"

"Richard Rosenberg wasn't involved in the case."

So. There it was, confirmation if I needed it, that Sergeant Thurman couldn't see beyond Richard Rosenberg.

"Yeah. Which is why I've been looking into people who are."

"Oh, I see. You're here to sell me on some whacky theory or other you dreamed up to help your boss. Nice try, but I'm not some credulous cop who's gonna fall for that shit. I've dealt with you before."

That was a surprise. Not that Sergeant Thurman didn't trust me—that he knew the word *credulous*.

"I wouldn't bullshit you, Thurman. I know you wouldn't fall for it. I'm giving you the straight stuff. The law clerk was involved with one of the ADAs on the Global Bank case. That made for a nice little romantic triangle, with Jeannie Atkins playing the part of the hypotenuse."

"Huh?"

"Not a Tom Lehrer fan?"

"Who?"

"The ADA's name is Edelstein. He and Richard were making a play for the same girl. That type of situation can turn ugly."

"She was cheating on him?"

"I'm sure that's how the ADA saw it."

"No, I mean she was cheating on Rosenberg."

I shrugged. "You pays your money and you takes your choice. The point is these things get messy, and sometimes things aren't as simple as you think they are."

"Sometimes they are."

That was hard to argue with. Sergeant Thurman, for instance, was as simple as I thought he was. But that's probably not what he meant.

"What's the ADA's name?"

"Edelstein. Working the Global Banking case. Presiding judge Peters. Jeannie Atkins was his law clerk."

"I know, I know."

It was nice that Thurman knew something. I hoped that wasn't the extent of it. I feared it was.

"As if that weren't complicated enough, the ADA's got a thing for one of the lawyers on the case too."

"He's gay?"

"No, there's a lady lawyer on the case."

"She hot?"

"Absolutely. And she might not take kindly to the competition."

"Interesting."

"I thought so. Anyway, I figured you might not have all of that."

"It's nice of you."

"Like I say, it's my duty."

"I thought you were just trying to get Richard Rosenberg off the hook."

"I *am* trying to get Richard Rosenberg off the hook. But I can't withhold things just because they implicate him."

"Good to know."

"Anything else I should work on?"

"I can't tell you about the case."

"I understand. I'm not asking you to. But if you tell me what you need to know, maybe I could help."

Thurman considered. "Rosenberg have a key?"

"To her apartment?"

"Yeah."

"What difference does it make? He was already there."

"I'd still like to know."

"I'll try to find out. Anything else?"

"Not at the moment."

"Okay. You think of anything, give me a call."

"What's your number."

I gave him my cell phone number. He wrote it in his notebook.

"Okay, thanks," he said. He shook my hand.

I was practically whistling as I went out the door. I couldn't believe how well it had gone.

If only there was a way to tell Richard.

19

"I asked MacAullif to talk to Thurman."

"And?"

"He still pegs you for it. As far as he's concerned, you're the guy."

"Shit."

"Well, we knew that."

"One can always hope."

"MacAullif get anything you could use?"

"No, but I figured it wouldn't be a bad idea to give Thurman a few leads."

"What do you mean?"

"About the other suspects."

"What other suspects?"

"The ADA and the lady lawyer."

"They're not suspects."

"They are now."

"You had MacAullif tell Thurman about the ADA and the lady lawyer?"

"Would that upset you?"

"It's not what I wanted."

"Then let's say he didn't."

"Stanley—"

"Hey. If you didn't want MacAullif to tell him, I don't wanna spoil your day. Did you want MacAullif to tell him or not?"

"I did not."

"Then he didn't."

"You can look me straight in the eye and say that?"

"I could look *Thurman* straight in the eye and say that. So let's say MacAullif *didn't* tell Thurman about the ADA and the lady lawyer. Let's just say Thurman got the idea."

Richard shook his head. "I can't believe how badly you've fucked this up. So MacAullif gave all that to Thurman and didn't get anything out of him?"

"We have the confirmation you're his only suspect."

"I could have told you that."

"We might have something else."

"What's that?"

"Thurman's interested in whether you had Jeannie's door key."

"MacAullif told you that?"

I frowned. "We have to have plausible deniability here. We're assuming Thurman told MacAullif nothing. We're assuming MacAullif told me nothing. Nonetheless, let's assume there's some interest in the door key."

"Why?"

"Don't look at me. I'm sure if there were a way MacAullif could have gotten that information, he would have. Care to enlighten me about the key?"

"Care to enlighten *me*? What the hell difference does it make to anyone whether or not I had a key?"

"It might piss off a jealous ADA."

"I thought Thurman didn't know about the jealous ADA. At least until MacAullif enlightened him."

"Right, he didn't. I don't know why Thurman cares about the key. Do you have one?"

"Why? So you can have MacAullif tell Thurman just in case there's any evidence against me he may have overlooked?"

"I wouldn't do that."

"Why? Not incriminating enough? He's not going to like you unless you bring him a signed confession?"

"So what's so important about the key?"

"You're asking me?"

"Why would Thurman be so concerned with whether you have one?"

"That's the question you should be asking. Instead of this other shit."

"So you admit it's a valuable point?"

"Valuable? It's crucial. You may well have cracked the case."

"Sorry I mentioned it."

"I'm not. It will give me something to think about for the rest of the afternoon."

"I just can't imagine why the key would be important. Do you need it to lock the door?"

"You need it to *open* the door."

"But you're already there. If Thurman's building a case against you, it's not like he has to show you had access to the apartment. You're already *in* the apartment."

"You expect me to argue?"

"No. I expect you to be as puzzled as I am."

"Fine. I'm stumped. What do you want with me?"

"You're good at cross-examining witnesses. You know their motivations. You figure out how they think."

"You see the fallacy there?"

"Right. Thurman doesn't think. But he has some motivation for what he does. He thinks you're guilty. He'll bend every fact to support that theory. For some reason or other, he thinks having a key would. What could you do with a key that you couldn't do if you didn't have a key? I'm assuming you lock the apartment door just by pulling it shut."

Richard sat bolt upright. "You *double*-lock it from the outside with a key!"

"Of course."

"Oh, fuck."

"That's gotta be it."

Richard shook his head. "No, it can't be."

"Why not?"

"Cops would have demanded it."

"Not with Thurman in charge."

"The ADA. If I didn't surrender it, they'd have got a warrant. But that didn't happen. They didn't even ask me. So it's gotta be something came up after."

"Like what?"

"I have no idea. I'll think about it. It just got dropped in my lap."

"Okay."

I got up to go. This time he didn't stop me. I smiled slightly as I headed for the door.

I did it. I managed to report the Sergeant Thurman situation without telling a single lie. Which was crucial. Richard Rosenberg is a human lie detector. The slightest falsehood registers in Richard's nervous system. Then he bores in for the kill. It's one of the things that makes him a demon cross-examiner. Witnesses are his meat. You can practically see him licking his chops. Opposing counsel who had been putting up a valiant fight would cave and talk their clients into settling the case after Richard had a go at their first witness. I was never comfortable when he questioned me about my job, even though I had done nothing wrong. Lying to the man was not an option. Nor was holding out on him. The only recourse was imparting all the necessary information while telling the absolute truth. And I'd done that. Tiptoed through a minefield. My relief was boundless.

He stopped me at the door. "Stanley."

"Yeah?"

"Next time you talk to Thurman, find out what's the deal with the key."

"Why do you need a key when you're already inside the apartment?"

MacAullif looked at me as if I were something he'd like to squash except that he didn't want to soil his shoe. "Is this a riddle?"

"It's a problem. Sergeant Thurman wants to know if Richard had a key to the apartment. Why would he need a key to the apartment when he's already *in* the apartment?"

"Who cares?"

"Thurman. It's the only thing he wanted."

"You spoke to Thurman?"

"Well, you wouldn't."

"Doesn't mean you should."

"I didn't know who else to ask. I figured it would be wimping out to send my wife."

"Thurman happy to see you?"

"About as happy as you are."

"He beat you up?"

"No."

"Then he's not as happy as I am."

While not exactly a threat, that wasn't really an invitation to come in and sit down.

"Thurman warmed up after I assured him I wasn't there to ask questions and fed him some information."

"You *gave* him some information?"

"Yeah."

"Why?"

"Figured he didn't have any."

"Probably a good guess. What'd you tell him?'

I gave MacAullif a rundown of my bullshit theories. I can't say he was impressed.

"Thurman buy that?"

"Well, he didn't push me through the wall."

"Yeah, well, he's not very bright. Wanna let me get back to work?"

"Not till you solve the key problem."

"Not my problem."

"It sort of is."

"Why?"

"I'm in your office."

MacAullif scowled, cocked his head. "Was the door double-locked when she was found."

"Couldn't have been."

"Why?"

"They'd have made Richard produce the key."

"Was he cooperating with the police?"

"No. He says they'd have got a warrant."

"Can't help you."

"Can't or won't?"

"Don't be a dickhead. I got no fuckin' idea why Thurman gives a shit about the goddamned key."

"You could find out."

"What?"

"Thurman won't tell me about it, but if a fellow officer—"

MacAullif rose from his chair like an avenging fury, two hundred and some-odd pounds of angry predator about to rip the limbs off its unsuspecting prey.

I figured that was probably a no on getting him to talk to Sergeant Thurman.

21

Alice was predictably supportive while snipping my balls off and displaying them in her trophy case for all the world to see.

She was in the kitchen chopping up some vegetables I'd never heard of to go with some grain I'd never heard of but was suddenly all the rage on the Upper West Side. The veggies and grain were to go with some meat I'd probably heard of but couldn't distinguish in the blend of onions and garlic and spices and wine in which it was happily burbling. It smelled good, but, then, as Alice will tell you, I don't know what good is.

She paused from her stirring long enough to say, "You did the best you could."

There it was. The totally supportive dagger through the heart. I had done the best I could. Which clearly wasn't good enough, but, hey, I gave it a shot. At the PI of the Year Awards I would be recognized for Best Effort. It stung a little, even after all these years.

"Well, what *should* I have done?" I said.

Alice didn't understand the question. "Nothing. You did everything you could."

"If I were more competent, what should I have done?"

Alice smiled. "If you were more competent, you'd know."

"Damn it."

"Stanley, relax. I'm not saying anyone could do any better."

"What *are* you saying?"

"You've done a great deal of work. It sounds like you've tried everything."

"Obviously not or I'd have some results."

"You found out Thurman's fixated on Richard."

"We knew that anyway."

"You have it confirmed. And you gave Thurman some new leads."

"He won't follow them."

"Yes, he will. He thinks they implicate Richard. A very clever idea on your part, giving him a lead he'd want to pursue."

"Not that there's anything to it."

"What?"

"The Bizarre Love Triangle."

"I thought it was a quadrangle."

"That's not the song."

"What song?"

"Off the *Married to the Mob* soundtrack. Same place you find 'Goodbye Horses.'"

"What?"

"The song Buffalo Bill dances to in *Silence of the Lambs*. Both movies were directed by Jonathan Demme, which is how 'Goodbye Horses' wound up on *Married to the Mob*."

Alice put down the spoon. "I always know you've really lost it when you start riffing on movie soundtracks. What are you doing?"

I was trying to steer the conversation away from an analysis of the merits of my investigation. By the time I got home I didn't want to talk about it anymore. But Alice was impatient to hear, what with Richard being involved and all.

I couldn't give her what she wanted, the slightest indication he might be innocent, and anything else seemed to elicit the type of approval that makes me want to slit my wrists.

Not that Alice was going to let it go. "You did all that yourself because MacAullif wouldn't lift a finger?"

"MacAullif's busy."

"He's been busy before and he's helped you. What's the matter, does he think Richard's guilty?"

That hadn't occurred to me. Was MacAullif's reluctance grounded in a firm belief that Richard might have done it? I didn't think so, but then I've been wrong on occasion. Just ask Alice.

"Alice, I don't know why MacAullif's not going to help me, but he's not going to help me. I know because I asked him again."

"When?"

"After I talked to Thurman."

"Why'd you go back?"

"To ask him to help."

"Why, if you knew he wouldn't?"

"I thought he might do it if it was something specific. Like if I had a theory I needed confirmed or disproved."

"What theory did you want proved?"

"No theory. Well, Thurman's theory."

"Which is what?"

"I don't know."

"Stanley."

I told Alice about Richard's key.

"Thurman wants to know if Richard had a key?"

"That's right."

"Why didn't Richard tell you that?"

"He didn't know."

"Huh?"

"Sometime after Richard was released, Thurman became interested in whether he had a key."

"He didn't drag him in and ask him?"

"Richard's not talking."

"Does Richard have a key?"

"That's not the point. The point is why Thurman wants to know. Richard thought maybe the door was double-locked from the outside."

Alice waved it away with the large metal spoon with which she was stirring the mixture on the stove. Miraculously, when Alice does something like that, nothing splatters. "If the door was double-locked, that's one of the first things the cops would have wanted to know. And he'd probably be in jail." She went back to stirring. "That's what you wanted MacAullif to ask Thurman?"

"Yeah?"

"Why do you have to ask him?"

"What do you mean?"

"Oh, come on. Thurman wants to know if Richard had a key and you want to know why that matters?"

"Yeah."

"So Richard could get back in after she was dead."

"So you could get in after she's dead."

Richard looked up from the newspaper he was reading. "Huh?"

"That's why Thurman wants to know about the key. Someone did something at the crime scene later that night. Well after the coroner said she died."

"I don't understand."

"Me either. 'Cause I don't know what it is. But there's your breakdown of Sergeant Thurman's thought process. There's an oxymoron. The cops found something that indicates someone did something at the crime scene well after the event. The cops figure whoever did must have a key."

"Aha," Richard said.

"So if you don't have a key, you're off the hook."

Richard frowned. "Not necessarily."

"Why do you say that?"

"Well, I could have taken her keys, used them to get in later, and put them back."

"But it had to be planned. You had to know you were going to come back when you left."

"There's another possibility."

"What's that?"

"I could have left the door unlocked. Easy enough to do. You just press the little button on the door that makes the outside knob turn when the door's shut. People do that when they go out in the hall in their pajamas to pick up the morning paper so they won't lock themselves out. Still, that's undoubtedly right, at least in terms of what Thurman wants. Did I have a key so I wouldn't have to do that? That's the way his mind works, so that's what he wants to know."

I wondered if Alice would be happy if she knew Richard had compared her thinking with Sergeant Thurman's.

"So," Richard said, "what else have you got?"

"What else?"

"Yeah."

"I would have thought this major breakthrough with the key would have merited some attention."

"Wasn't I appreciative enough? Good work, Stanley. I'm tremendously relieved. Yes, my girlfriend was murdered and the police think I did it, but, hey, my ace investigator may have actually figured something out."

"I haven't figured anything out. I thought you might be of some help as to what there was in Jeannie Atkins's apartment that might have given someone a reason to want to get in after she was dead."

"You're convinced such a thing exists?"

"If it doesn't, I don't understand."

"Like that's a deal breaker? Stanley, I'm sorry I don't attach more importance to your marvelous deduction."

"Actually, it's my wife's deduction. I hate to have to tell her you pooh-poohed it."

"Ah, the plaintive cry of the terminally pussy whipped. And you wonder why I'm still a bachelor."

"Because you keep killing your girlfriends?"

Richard's mouth fell open. "What are you trying to do, shock me into sincerity? I'm not up to sincerity, and I don't think I'll be functioning on that front for some time. My life's been ripped from under me, I'm at a complete loss as to what's happening, I have an amazing repertoire of legal skills, and they don't help me. Nothing helps me. A little clarity might be nice, but that seems like the impossible dream. So let me answer your question seriously and with all due consideration. No. There is nothing in Jeannie's apartment that someone would need to come back for after she was dead. Unless the killer left something in the apartment, and how would Thurman know that if it was left and then taken? What would be the evidence of that?"

Richard cocked his head, back in control. "I know what you're hoping for. The body was stuffed in a Deepfreeze™ to alter the time of death, and the killer had to come back hours later, take it out, and arrange the crime scene so as to look natural."

"Did she have a Deepfreeze™?"

"Don't be an idiot! I was using that as an absurd example."

I knew that. I'd just said it help snap him out of sincerity. I'd asked for it, but it was too damn depressing.

Of course, once Richard brought it up, I could think of nothing else.

23

"Did she have a Deepfreeze™?"

Sergeant Thurman's nose crinkled up. "Huh?"

"The victim. Jeannie Atkins. Did she have a Deepfreeze™ in her apartment?"

"How the hell should I know?"

"You searched the crime scene."

"I didn't search it for ice cream."

"Yeah, but you're observant. Let's put it this way. Did she have anything in her apartment that wasn't in the other apartments?"

"A dead body."

I figured I could pretty well wash out the alter-the-time-of-death-by-refrigeration theory as far as Sergeant Thurman was concerned. So whether there was a Deepfreeze™ in the apartment or not, it had nothing to do with why Thurman wanted to know if Richard had a key to the apartment.

Which didn't keep me from wanting to pursue the subject. Just because Sergeant Thurman hadn't thought of it didn't mean it wasn't true.

Luckily there were other means of obtaining the information.

The doorman, for instance, still thought I was a cop.

I must say Ramon Castella looked a lot better in uniform than he had in his apartment. Gussied up in a ritzy East Side doorman's outfit, complete with gold braid, he looked like just the type of snooty tight ass who would be delighted to deny you access.

Not that he was about to deny me. I was a presumed cop.

"What do you want?" he said. Not as cordial as if I'd looked rich, not as condescending as if I were a deliveryman but still managing to convey the impression he wished I were somewhere else.

"Did the deceased have a Deepfreeze™ in her apartment?"

"Why?"

"We'd like to know."

I'm not sure if you can be convicted for impersonating an officer by using the plural pronoun, but that's certainly the way the doorman heard it.

"I thought we were done with you guys. You released the crime scene so we could start renovating the apartment."

"What's to renovate?"

"Probably nothing. But they send in a work crew to make whatever repairs are necessary. Most likely plaster and paint."

"Have they started?"

"How could they? You just released it."

"I didn't release it. I didn't even know it had been done. So, did she have a Deepfreeze™?"

"I don't know. She'd been in there for years. I don't recall one being delivered, but it's not that big a deal. It also could have happened on my day off. It's a one-bedroom, so you wouldn't expect a Deepfreeze™. A larger apartment with a maid's room, it would be much more likely."

"But the renovations haven't started?"

"No."

"So it wouldn't have been moved out?"

"No. Why would it?"

"If it's valuable, someone might have wanted to sell it."

His eyes shifted slightly.

Oh, my god! Had the doorman and the super been involved in selling appliances out of the vacated apartments? Yet another absurd possibility to nag at me.

"No, no one could have sold anything out of the apartment. You just released it as a crime scene. And who's going to be stupid enough to sell something that's probably been inventoried by the police? Of course, if you don't know, maybe it *hasn't* been inventoried by the police, but who would know that?"

He'd obviously given it some consideration, but that was the extent of it. His guilty reaction to selling off appliances was not because he'd sold Jeannie Atkins's Deepfreeze™, merely that it was the type of activity that he would have engaged in.

I heaved a sigh. "I guess I'll have to go see. Anyone up there now?"

"Shouldn't be."

"I'll need the key."

"I don't have it."

"Don't give me a hard time. If a tenant's not responding, you got a passkey to go in and check. You don't break down the door."

"That's not me. That's the super."

"He has the key?"

"That's right."

"Where will I find him?"

The super looked like selling dead tenants' appliances was the legitimate end of his business, a front he used as a cover for trafficking in teen prostitution and drugs. Of course I was making all that up. The guy was most likely a perfectly respectable family man whose wife and three kids lived in a walk-up on the West Side furnished by a lifetime of dedication and hard work. Nonetheless, the bleary-eyed gentleman in the rumpled work shirt who had only managed to half-zip his pants did not inspire confidence.

I phrased the question carefully. "I know Jeannie Atkins's apartment has been released as a crime scene, but I gotta get in there and check something out. You wanna go up there and open it for me or you wanna give me the key?"

He gave me the key. I had to ask him what apartment, but that didn't seem to bother him. Nothing seemed to bother him, as long as I wasn't there to bust him.

Jeannie Atkins lived in 14C, a modest apartment by any standards. It didn't even have a Central Park view, the main selling point of a Fifth Avenue address. It had a short foyer that segued directly into the living room, with a side door off to a rather small kitchen, large enough for a full-size fridge but nowhere to put a Deepfreeze™.

Nor was there room anywhere else in the apartment, unless you wanted to move out a queen-sized bed. I tried not to think of what went on in that bed. Neither sex with Richard nor murder were easy to take. The bed had been stripped. The mattress was stained with what was probably blood.

The murder weapon had come from the kitchen. I checked it out. There was a rack of steak knives on the counter. One knife was missing.

I was free to search the apartment. Of course, I didn't know what I was looking for. But it was probably my only chance. Once the renovation crews moved in, there would be nothing left.

I went through her dresser drawers. They were full. No relative had cleaned them out. I wondered if that was significant.

Her diaphragm was in the top drawer. I wondered if she still used it. She hadn't put it in for Richard. But then the semen was external. I wondered if that was always the case. I wondered if there would come a time when I'd have to ask Richard.

There was nothing else of note in the drawer, unless you count the sheer thong panties. I did but not in terms of the murder investigation.

The second drawer held pullover tops. They suggested someone still young, playful.

The drawer below held shorts and slacks.

The bottom drawer held sweaters.

So much for the dresser.

I continued my search of the apartment. Found nothing. At least nothing that would help.

There was nothing in the kitchen cupboards, nothing in the cookie jar. No diamonds frozen in the ice cubes. Though if there were, I'm not sure I'd be able to spot them.

There was nothing under the sofa cushions, nothing under the rug. No sealed plastic bags floating in the tank top of the toilet. Just looking for them made me realize I was starting to lose it.

I went back into the bedroom, searched the dresser again. There was nothing in the pockets of the clothes. I pulled the drawers all the way out of the dresser, searched behind them. Was not surprised to find nothing. I replaced the drawers. Realized I should have looked on the bottom. Which would be awkward, unless I emptied them. I pulled the panties drawer out, bent down, looked underneath.

There was something there!

I dropped to the floor. Looked up. Sure enough, there was a manila envelope taped to the bottom of the drawer. It was held in place by strips of masking tape.

I reached up, pulled them down. I tried to do it calmly without tearing. It wasn't easy.

I pulled the tape free and stood up.

I unclasped the envelope. Was immediately disappointed. I had hoped for a letter. But there was no paper in the envelope.

It was empty.

I squeezed the envelope so that it bulged open, looked inside.

It wasn't empty!

A small square of paper, not much more than an inch wide, was in the bottom.

I reached in, pulled it out.

It wasn't square, it was slightly rectangular.

There was something written on it.

I turned it over.

Printed on the paper was the numeral twelve.

"Do you know what twelve is?"

"Huh?"

"The numeral twelve. Do you know what it is?"

"A dozen."

"Besides that."

"Stanley, have you lost your mind?"

"No, I'm trying to help you. Right now I need to know if the number twelve means anything to you."

"Why?"

I opened my briefcase, pulled out the manila envelope with the masking tape still clinging to it, dropped it on Richard's desk, and walked out.

He caught up with me in the foyer.

"Stanley!" he bellowed.

Janet/Wendy, at the switchboard, froze. The expression on her face was priceless. She couldn't imagine how badly I must have fucked up to warrant this.

I turned around. "Yes?"

"Get in here!"

I went back into Richard's office, sat down in front of his desk. He didn't sit, just stood behind his desk chair glaring down at me. He pointed to the envelope. The slip of paper lay next to it. "What the hell is this?"

"The number twelve."

"I know it's the number twelve. Where did you get it?"

"Taped to the underside of Jeannie Atkins's panty drawer."

I don't think Richard could have been more surprised had I put on Jeannie Atkins's panties and danced around the office.

"How the hell did you get that?"

I told him about getting the passkey.

"You impersonated a police officer?"

"I did nothing of the sort."

"You represented yourself as one."

"Absolutely not. I just asked for the key to the apartment."

"Which the super gave you, because he thought you were a police officer."

"I'm not responsible for what the super thought."

"In the case of impersonating a police officer, you are."

"And you would be able to demonstrate that I didn't. You're telling me you couldn't poke holes in that theory? You could do it in your sleep."

"Which doesn't mean I want to. The police would like to make a case against me for murder. Anything that prods them in that direction is bad. Whether or not it is technically defensible is of little consequence."

"Not to me."

Richard sat down at his desk. "All right. You finessed your way into the apartment. You're proud of yourself. You feel like the hero in some pulp fiction novel."

"And I found something the police didn't."

"So you think."

"Huh?"

Richard pointed to the envelope on the desk. "How do you know that isn't something the police planted just to see if we'd start messing in the case? If we start showing an interest in the number twelve, they'll figure we did. Finding the envelope gone will confirm it."

"Do you really think they did that?"

"No," Richard said. "But now that I mentioned it, you will. That's the way your mind works. Totally convoluted. Let's assume the envelope is real."

"I am. That's why I'm asking you. Did the number twelve mean anything to Jeannie?"

"Not that I know of."

"Then why would it be there?"

"I have no idea."

"It's not handwritten, it's printed. On a little square of paper."

"It's actually sort of rectangular," Richard said. "Look at it. Isn't it a little wider than it is high?" He chuckled "Do you know what it looks like?"

"What?"

"An inspection tag."

"What's that?"

"You know. You buy a brand name shirt or pants, find it in the pocket. 'Inspected by 9.' That's the number of the inspector who inspected that lot of clothing."

"It doesn't say 'inspected by.'"

"No, it just says twelve. I don't think that's a deal breaker. The product could use just the number as a shorthand."

I looked at Richard. "You really believe that?"

"What else could it be?"

"It could be like that old admiral."

"What old admiral?"

"Famous old admiral. Legendary. Had a huge safe on the bridge. Every day he got up, opened it, took out a piece of paper, looked at it, locked it back up again. Everyone wanted to know what it said, because they figured it was the secret to his success. When he died, the first thing they did was open the safe, take out the paper."

"What did it say?"

"Starboard is right, port is left."

"That's an old joke."

"I thought you hadn't heard it."

"You don't have to have heard it to know it's old. Is there a point to this?"

"What if that's all this was?"

Richard blinked. "You think Jeannie might forget the number twelve?"

"I never met Jeannie."

"You think *anyone* might forget the number twelve?"

"The last week it could have been eight. And the week before it was eleven. Like it's a passcode for something and you need to be up on the current version. The most recent was twelve."

"Your theories aren't getting better, they're getting worse."

"All right," I said. "What if it is starboard is right, port is left? She's clerking for a judge. What if she has to reassure herself how many people there are on a jury?"

"Why?"

"I don't know. Maybe her job was to order them lunch."

"There's more than twelve people on a jury. There's the alternates."

"Right. I was an alternate myself once."

"I can't believe we're talking about this. The number twelve doesn't matter. It's probably just an inspection certificate. The envelope most likely had something else in it. In which case, the killer probably got it."

I snapped my fingers. "That's it."

"What?"

"That's what the killer needed a key to come back and get."

"Because taking it the first time would have been too easy," Richard said witheringly.

"Because he didn't dare stay there then for fear of being spotted. Maybe he had an accomplice. Someone called him on the phone, said that that Rosenberg guy's driver just turned his car around, he may be headed back."

"He didn't turn my car around."

"That was just an example."

"It was just a bad example. If you wanna keep coming up with theories that aren't true, don't be surprised if I don't think very much of them."

"All right, fine," I said, "but by rights what was in the envelope should have something to do with the key to the apartment."

"Rights?"

"Well, we have two unexplained things. It would be nice if they explained each other."

Richard heaved a huge sigh. "Life isn't nice."

#

Richard had not explicitly forbade me from asking people about the number 12. He had pointed out how bad it would be if the police had left it as bait just to see if we'd take it. But I didn't believe that was true. And if it was, I wanted to know it. Of course, watching them arrest Richard would have been a less than triumphant confirmation. Nonetheless, Richard was in trouble, and I just couldn't sit on my hands.

When court recessed for lunch the next day, I wandered up behind the attractive defense attorney and said, "Twelve."

The look she gave me was priceless. First of all was the fact she gave me a look. Before that, I had been the invisible man, the type of guy an attractive woman doesn't look at. But aside from that, there was a look of puzzlement on her face, as well as a slight trace of fear.

You must understand: I'm not a scary guy. A genial personality, coupled with a lifetime of assuring potential clients that the injury they had suffered would be well taken care of in our hands, I presented as pretty benign. And I was wearing a suit and tie, as per my job, perhaps not as flashy as an attorney billing out at fifteen hundred an hour but not the type to get you thrown out of a nice restaurant either. So there was no reason for her to be scared of me. Particularly in a public setting like a courthouse. It wasn't like she was defending Jack the Ripper and a host of victims' relatives were hanging out in court every day clamoring for her blood.

But there it was. She looked at me, I smiled, she looked away. Then walked away. Rather more quickly than I would have thought the situation would demand.

Interesting. I wondered if she would tell the young ADA. If she did, I wondered if the young ADA would tell Thurman. Well, not Thurman. But the ADA handling Richard's case. Who may or may not have let Thurman in on the gag. Though you would think he would have to, because someone would have to plant the envelope. I couldn't see the ADA himself doing it.

I wondered if I should ask him. But he and the other ADA had already left. Instead, I tried the law clerks. Dorky Clerk said, "Huh?" Plain Jane said, "We're having lunch at noon?" Neither came accompanied by a guilty reaction, confirming my opinion that that attractive defense attorney's reaction might mean something.

On the other hand, they knew me and she didn't, which might make a difference. I'd have to test that theory on someone else.

One of the other defense attorneys was standing near the rail. I walked up to him, said, "Twelve."

He eyed me with contempt. "That's not the way to plea-bargain."

That caught me up short. That wasn't the way to plea-bargain? I never thought it was. What did he think, I was offering a twelve-year sentence for a guilty plea? How did that compute? The guy knew I wasn't an ADA. Did he think maybe I was the consigliore, some superattorney the DA sent in to handle crucial negotiations?

I wasn't quite sure what my next move was. I shrugged, said, "Suit yourself," and walked off. Which was probably as good a move as any. There was nothing I could say that wasn't going to get me into trouble.

I turned back in the doorway to see if the guy was still watching. But he was having a rather intense conversation in low voices with the other male attorney, whom he'd pulled out of earshot. I wondered if he was asking his buddy if he'd been offered twelve years to have his client roll over on him.

Which was good, because the day hadn't started well. Testimony was boring. It was a bunch of financial stuff I didn't understand. I don't fault myself for that, however. One would have had to have been trained as a certified public accountant, then locked in a dungeon for twenty years with nothing to read but the figures relating to this case. I didn't have a clue what was going on. The fact the attorneys were able to frame questions was extraordinary. And the ability to understand the answers seemed superhuman. The wonder was that a grand jury had been able to sift through enough of this to render a verdict. I figured they probably had indicted the defendants out of self-defense, just to make the whole thing stop.

Anyway, we had broken for lunch early, and no one seemed disappointed when we did.

I was contemplating my next move when the bailiff made it for me. "Mr. Hastings?"

"Yes."

"Judge Peters wants to see you in his chambers."

The judge was eating a ham sandwich when I came in. I smiled at that. The judge didn't miss much or let much go by. "What are you smiling at?"

"Your ham sandwich. I wondered if they'd indicted it."

"Oh, that old saw. You could get the grand jury to indict a ham sandwich. It's not true, by the way. We've had feisty grand jurors in some cases."

"What happens then?"

"They usually get outvoted by the other jurors."

"And the ham sandwich goes to trial."

"Well, if it wasn't guilty, it wouldn't have been charged. Any more defense gripes you'd like to air?"

"No. You wanted to see me, Your Honor?"

"I can't believe you're interested in the financial structure of Global Bank."

"I can't believe you managed to stay awake."

"It's my job. I'm wondering why it's yours."

"Are you suggesting it's none of my business?"

"I'm just curious."

"The Case of the Curious Judge. Sounds like a Perry Mason novel."

"I'm not kidding. If something's going on in my courtroom, I wanna know."

"You do know. I'm investigating the case of your law clerk."

"By watching my trial?"

"You got a better lead?"

"I don't have any leads at all. I hope Richard Rosenberg is innocent, but I don't have any idea who's guilty. I can see you checking out the case she was on. I can't see you coming back."

I looked at my watch. "It's nearly twelve."

He frowned. "Got an appointment?"

"No, but I've got a watch."

The frown became a scowl. "I have heard you're brighter than you look. You would almost have to be. So let me ask you: Are you *trying* to irritate me?"

"Not at all. I'm trying to make some sense out of an impossible situation. I don't have much to go on, so I poke and prod."

"You consider me a suspect?"

"I don't know you. You're a judge. One would think that would exclude you, but in a murder case it doesn't. Murder crosses all social boundaries. So please don't take it personally. I happen to like you."

"I'm delighted to hear it."

"Now, then, you may not like me, but would you like to help me?"

"How?"

"Tell me something. Would a romance between an ADA and a defense attorney be a conflict of interest?"

"Of course it would."

"How about a romance between an ADA and a judge's law clerk?"

"Are you trying to tell me something?"

"I'm trying not to tell you something. And I doubt if you're eager, after umpteen weeks of this mind-numbing testimony, to declare a mistrial and start again. And I see no reason you should have to do that. But if I should find one in the course of my investigation, would you want to know?"

He hesitated.

I grinned. "I retract the question. You don't want to say yes and get that information. And you can't say no and go on record that you prefer to ignore it. So let's pretend I never asked."

There was a knock on the judge's door.

The bailiff came in. "Sorry to interrupt, Your Honor. Juror number nine is sick."

Judge Peters snorted in disgust. "How sick?"

"Fever, chills, diarrhea."

"You feel his forehead?"

"No."

"But this is what he claims?"

"Yes, Your Honor."

"Just came on him during lunch break?"

"He said he hasn't felt well all morning, could hardly wait for you to recess."

"We're already two alternates down."

"I know."

"We can't afford to lose another one. All right, we'll adjourn for the day. Send him to the doctor. Tomorrow morning at ten o'clock I want him back here ready to serve or with a letter from his doctor stating he's too sick to sit in court, what he has, and how long he's likely to be out. If he agrees to that, he can leave now; I'll send everybody else home after lunch."

"Yes, Your Honor."

As the bailiff went out I said, "What do you mean you lost two alternates?"

"We started the case with four. Two jurors have already dropped out, so we're down to two. If I lose one now we'll be down to one, and that's just cutting it too thin."

"Do you really think the juror's faking?"

Judge Peters cocked his head. "You heard the testimony. Would you want to hear any more?"

26

Alice was designing me a website when I got home. She'd registered the domain name stanleyhastings.com, so no one else could take it as their website. I now had it as mine, which was wonderful, except there was absolutely nothing I needed a website for.

There should have been. I started out as an actor and a writer, failed in both fields. My last acting job was a summer stock production of *Arms and the Man*, where I got shoehorned into the cast because the leading man dropped dead during rehearsal, and I'd done the show before and knew the part. And my only writing work was the screenplay for a Jason Clairemont martial arts movie. Somehow all that didn't warrant a website, and I took Alice's insistence that I have one as a passive-aggressive way of underlining the fact I didn't need one.

Nonetheless, she was having a good time with Photoshop and Adobe or whatever the hell those programs were that allowed you design things electronically, then play with them, changing size and color and brightness and contrast. Alice had a zillion things to work with.

Except content. She was rather lean on content, though she seemed to be making do.

"So what are you working on now?" I said.

"Video page."

"Video page?"

"Movie clips."

I shouldn't have been surprised. *Hands of Havoc, Flesh of Fire* was out on DVD. It was easy enough for Alice to capture clips, stick 'em up on YouTube, and put links on the website. As I watched, I saw a younger version of my buddy, Sergeant MacAullif, typecast as a cop, patrolling Needle Park, back before it was rebuilt as part of the 72nd Street subway station, and interacting with a prison escapee, played by Jason Clairemont.

"Can't you get in trouble with that?"

"With whom?" Alice said.

"The movie studio."

"Bring it on!" Alice said. "Think of the publicity. Major motion picture studio takes on poor, defenseless screenwriter. It's a real David and Goliath story."

"I don't have a slingshot."

"You're too literal."

"And what am I going to do with this publicity? I have nothing to sell."

"Well, you should. Take some of your old writing and put it on Kindle."

"I don't have any old writing."

"What about the screenplay?"

"I wrote it for hire."

"Not *that* screenplay. The legal thriller."

"It wasn't a thriller."

"It will be when you publish it. You gotta put it in categories. That's your category. Legal thrillers."

"It's formatted like a screenplay."

"You think I can't format a screenplay for Kindle?"

"I'm sure you can. But no one's gonna read one."

"You're wrong, they will. But if you don't want to publish it as a screenplay, just edit it. Change the dialogue headings into he says and she says and the stage directions into description."

"That doesn't make a novel."

"Sure, it does. Writers do novelizations of movies all the time."

"I can't just knock things out. I'd have to start from scratch and type the whole thing again."

"No, you won't. I scanned your screenplay into Microsoft Word. You'll have to fix a few typos, and you can edit it on the computer just as if you'd typed it in to begin with."

"You're kidding."

Alice smiled. "Stanley, you've really gotta keep up with the times."

"You can really do that?"

"I can and I did and it's a Word document, and you can work on it anytime you want."

"Where is it?"

Alice clicked on the Word icon. A menu of documents filled the screen. "Right here. See, I pinned it so it will be easy to find."

"Pinned it?"

She moved the mouse, pointed with the cursor. "This little pin here. It will always be near the top of the list, with the other pinned documents."

Alice clicked on it. The first page of my long-forgotten screen-play filled the screen. "So, whip that into a book and publish it on Kindle."

"How much does it cost?"

"If I do the formatting, nothing. If I design the cover, the only cost is any stock photo or graphic we may want to use. Anyway, this has never been published or produced, so you're free to change the title or anything else you want."

"Why would I change the title?"

"I'm doing a survey on what sells, particularly among self-published books. No reason not to benefit from experience."

"Alice, I'm a little overwhelmed. I just came from watching real legal proceedings. Richard is facing real legal proceedings. I'm not sure I'm up to dealing with fictional law at the moment."

"Yeah, I know," Alice said. "You're home early. How'd it go?"

I told her about dropping hints about the number twelve.

"Richard told you not to but you're doing it anyway?"

"I figure Richard's not necessarily the best authority, being personally involved."

"You could also say his wishes should be respected for the same reason."

"You think I shouldn't do it?"

"I didn't say that."

"Well, what are you saying?"

"I don't know. Just if this blows up and hurts Richard, you're gonna be hard to live with."

"I'm sorry, but Richard's in serious trouble. I wasn't really thinking of your feelings."

"That wasn't what I meant and you know it. So, did your probing meet with any success?"

"The attractive ADA seemed uncomfortable."

"Well, why not? She's being hit on by a dirty old man. Did you breathe on her shoulder and whisper the word *twelve* in a husky voice?"

"I was a perfect gentleman."

"There you are. That would frighten anyone."

"It did have one curious side effect."

"What's that?"

"The judge invited me into his chambers."

"Really? How come?"

"He wanted to know what I was doing."

"Did you tell him?"

"Not specifically."

"I didn't think so. Or he'd have wanted to know where you got the idea. He wouldn't think you'd burglarized the apartment. He'd have assumed you got it from Richard. Not exactly the impression you wanted to convey."

I sighed. "I know."

"And did the judge bar you from the courtroom?"

"Why would he do that?"

"I don't know. But you're home early."

"One of the jurors got sick. They had to adjourn court."

"Oh. And then the judge invited you into his chambers."

"No. That was when they broke for lunch. We were still talking when the bailiff came in to say one of the jurors was sick."

"Interesting. What's his name?"

"The bailiff?"

"The sick juror."

"Why?"

"I would think you'd want to know. With your conspiracy theory mind. Make sure he's really sick. That someone didn't get to him."

"The judge took care of that."

"Oh?"

"The juror has to show up in court with a doctor's letter stating the reason he should be excused or he has to serve."

"Well, that's good. What's his name?"

"I don't know."

"You didn't think it was important enough to remember his name?"

114

"The bailiff didn't say."

"The bailiff didn't tell the judge which juror was sick?"

"Yeah, but they don't use names. He just said juror number nine."

"Well, there you are."

"Where am I?"

"There's your answer."

"Alice."

"Stanley, wake up. I ask you the juror's name, you don't know, you just know it's juror nine."

"So?"

"So what's the question you need to ask?"

"Who's juror nine?"

"Don't be silly. Who's juror twelve?"

27

She was a dish. How did I miss her before? Pouty lips, auburn hair. Little ski-jump nose. Languid brown eyes framed by long lashes. Curvy cashmere sweater. All heaven in a day.

It occurred to me I was not going to be happy reporting to Alice who juror number twelve was.

Though I might enjoy interviewing her.

For my money, she wasn't that interested in the case. Not that that made her special. The number of jurors who were interested in the case could be counted on the fingers of no hands. Nonetheless, auburn babe was bored.

Juror nine was there, by the way. His doctor hadn't come through. I wondered if the good doctor had had a phone call from the judge, or from one of the judge's law clerks, implying that if the doctor was serious about keeping juror nine from attending the rest of the trial, it might require a personal appearance in court for him to attest to the fact. For whatever reason, a medical discharge was not forthcoming, and juror nine was there.

The juror in question was a young man in a sports shirt and slacks who gave every appearance of being the picture of health. Not that that precluded some mystery ailment that might fell him at any moment, but if he had one the doctor hadn't found it. He sat there in court looking as bored as the rest and slightly miffed. I wondered if he'd take it out in the verdict. And if so, against whom?

If the judge noticed me sitting there, he gave no sign. Still, I wondered if I'd be receiving a summons at recess.

Midmorning we broke for half an hour. I watched the jurors file out, wondered how I was going to get to them. They wouldn't be going anywhere but the jury room. It occurred to me I was going to have to be colossally lucky. Not my default position.

"You're a private eye!"

The Plain Jane law clerk had slid into the seat next to me. Her eyes were shining, and I was afraid she might swoon. She looked like she had just met James Bond.

Oh, dear. I smiled self-deprecatingly. "That's misleading. I chase ambulances."

She waved it away. "No, you don't. Lawyers chase ambulances."

"Yes, but the successful ones don't chase them themselves. They hire someone to do it."

"Right. A private eye."

"That's not the point. The point is I'm not here as a private investigator. Only as a concerned friend."

"Friend?"

"My friend was dating Jeannie Atkins. He wants to know what happened."

She sighed in disgust. "Of course he was."

"What do you mean?"

"*Everyone* was dating Jeannie Atkins. That's the type of girl she was. You know. Loose. Coquette." She gestured in the direction of the other law clerk. "Don't tell him I said so. He won't see it. Guys don't."

"You mean Jeannie was involved with someone else?"

"Involved? *Involved* isn't the right word. Jeannie made a play for everyone. And they never even knew it. A smile, a simper, a bat of eyelashes. She had those guys wrapped around her finger."

"But specifically. Was there anyone who was more than that?"

"Stu."

"Stu?"

"The ADA. The young one. They were hot and heavy until he broke it off."

"He broke it off?"

"She wouldn't. She liked to keep 'em dangling. That's the type of girl she was."

"You sound like you're not unhappy she's gone."

"Well, I didn't want her killed. Just stopped. You know how depressing it is to watch the teacher's pet get answer after answer right?"

"So he broke it off."

"That's right."

"How do you know?"

"How do I know anything? He stopped seeing her. He got interested in someone else."

"Who was that?"

"The defense attorney. It's funny to watch 'em. They try to be discreet, but they're not."

"How come you didn't tell me this at lunch?"

"Lunch?"

"The first day. When I took you guys out for cheeseburgers."

"I didn't know you. I wasn't sure if I should."

"Have you told the judge?"

"Not my place."

"It sort of is."

She immediately began to backtrack. "Hold on there. If I told the judge he'd have to take action. It would come out it was me. He'd tell people what I said. He'd make me testify, if it came to that. And it would come to that, if the bar association got involved. I told you in confidence. You're not going to repeat what I said. I'll deny it if you do."

"I'm not going to tell the judge. You don't betray my confidence, I won't betray yours."

She liked that. The idea of having the inside track with a PI was a thrill. I thanked my profession for the undeserved boost.

"So, Jeannie was hot and heavy with the ADA, but he broke it off because he got interested in the defense attorney. Right?"

"That's right."

"So was she involved with anyone else? Beyond a casual flirtation, I mean."

She glanced around. "Once again, you didn't hear it from me."

"Didn't hear what from you?"

"This is really hush-hush. I don't think anyone has the slightest inkling."

"About what?"

"I think she was making a play for the jurors."

"You're kidding."

"No."

"Who?"

"I don't know. But I'm sure she was."

"How can you know if you don't know who?"

She put up her hand. "It sounds whacky. But I'm not crazy. She was more interested in the jury than she had any right to be. Like, take ordering lunch. She'd volunteer when it wasn't her turn. Nobody volunteers, particularly not for that. It's a shit detail. Always some diva with a special request off the menu. And then when they won't fill it, it's your fault."

"So you didn't mind giving up your shift."

"Hey, if she wanted to order lunch, that was fine with me. The point is, she made excuses to be with the jury."

"But you don't know who in particular."

"Gotta be one of the guys. She was boy crazy."

"Was she hitting on the other law clerk?"

She made a face. "You met him. Give me a break. But there was something about the jurors. Trust me on this."

"Interesting," I said. I lowered my voice confidentially. "Listen, keep your eyes open, let me know if you see anything I should know."

I excused myself, went out into the corridor to lie in wait for juror twelve. Which was, I knew, a losing proposition. In all probability I'd have to wait until they went home.

A court officer with a file of papers was coming in my direction. I stopped him and said, "Excuse me, where's the jury room?"

"You can't go in there."

"I know. I want to be sure to avoid it."

He gave me a look. "You can't see the jury. Don't hang out in the corridor."

"Sorry," I said. "I'm going to the restroom. I don't want to walk through the wrong door."

"Can you read the word *Men*?" He pointed. "Down the hall on the right."

"Thanks."

I availed myself of the facilities, came back out. I wondered where the ladies' room was. I wondered if juror twelve might want to use it. I realized she wouldn't. There were bathroom facilities right in the jury room. There was no reason in the world for her to come out.

So she did.

Not only that, she came out alone. I would have hated to have to cull her from the herd. But there she was, striding down the corridor, as if in search of a ladies' room, which I knew she wasn't.

I fell in step beside her and said, "Juror Twelve, I presume."

She stopped, stared at me. "I beg your pardon?"

"Sorry. I don't know your name. But you are juror number twelve."

"Who are you?"

"I've been watching the trial."

"I can't talk about the trial."

"I know that. I'm not from the press."

"I can't talk about it to anyone."

"I know. I don't want to talk about the trial."

That did not reassure her. Anything but.

"Hey," I said, "I'm not dangerous. You wanna sit down on that bench over there, give me five minutes of your time, you can get up any time you want."

"Look, I'm on my way to the bathroom."

"I thought you had one in the jury room."

"Like I'm going to wait for that."

"Fine. Go on. Go. Come back, take five minutes to satisfy your curiosity."

"*My* curiosity?"

"Sure. You must wanna know what I'm after. It's not just that you're very pretty. Believe me, this is not a new way to pick up girls."

She looked at me as if I were from Mars, then stomped off to the bathroom.

I gave it a 50-50 shot. She would have to be, as I said, curious. Just telling her she'd be curious would make her curious. Or so I figured. And I can't be wrong all the time, no matter what Alice says.

I lucked out. She was back five minutes later and said, "Okay, what do you want?"

I gestured to the bench in the hallway. There was no one near.

"Fine," she said.

We went over to the bench and sat down.

"I don't know what you think about the case," I said. "I'll tell you what I think about the case. It's the most boring case I've ever heard. And I've sat on a couple of juries. If I had to sit on this one I'd slit my wrists."

"I see. You came to give me a pep talk."

"Not exactly."

"You trying to talk me off the jury?"

"Why, has that happened?"

"Not to me."

"You mean it happened to someone else?"

"Hey, no one has to talk anyone off this jury. They're fighting to get off."

"Yeah. Like Juror nine. Was he sick at all?"

She looked at me suspiciously. "You're here to make trouble for him?"

"Is there any reason he should be in trouble?"

"No."

"Then I don't see how I could."

"Glib, wiseass answers like that don't make me want to help you. Start making sense or I'm walking away."

"Jeannie Atkins."

"Who?"

"You don't know Jeannie Atkins?"

"Is that the girl who got killed?"

"The law clerk."

"Is that her?"

"Yeah, that's her. You didn't know her?"

"I know the name. That's the law clerk who got killed."

"You never met her?"

"I probably saw her. I don't remember her. When they said a law clerk had been killed, I didn't know who. Since then I've noticed the ones who are alive. That doesn't help me remember the one that's dead."

She seemed sincere. If she was lying, she was damn good. I couldn't see it, and I was looking for it. Had been from the minute I mentioned the name. There was no reaction. Her first automatic impulse was *who?*

"Any of the other jurors know her?"

"How would I know?"

"I'd think it would be the topic of conversation. Someone associated with the case got killed. Someone would say, oh, my god, Ben, you knew her, didn't you?"

"Ben?"

"A name at random. I don't know any of the jurors."

"Why are you interested in the law clerk?"

"I'm not. I'm interested in who killed her."

"You with the police?"

"No."

"Then why?"

"A friend of mine knew her. He wants to know."

"A friend?"

"Yeah."

"You're not being paid?"

"No."

That was technically true. Richard hadn't authorized what I was doing, so I could hardly bill him for it. On the other hand, if it should turn out to be valuable . . .

"Who's your friend?"

"If he wanted to be known he'd be here."

She shook her head. "I can't help you. I don't know her, and I don't know anyone who knew her. You might try the other jurors."

"Any in particular?"

"I have no idea. You might try Ron. He hits on anything in a skirt."

"Who's Ron?"

"Juror number four."

"Could you point him out to me?"

"I could, but I'm not gonna. I don't want to give him a reason to talk to me. Not that he needs one. But why ask for it. I don't have to, though. He'll be the fourth juror in the first row."

She got up, smiled, said, "Sorry I'm no help," and walked off.

I wouldn't say no help. She had given me a lead. Ron. Of course I'd have to wait until court resumed to spot him. And he wasn't juror twelve. He was juror four. I didn't want juror four to be important. That didn't do anything for my theories. Of course you have to take what you can get.

I wandered back to the courtroom to see if anyone would spirit me off to the judge's chambers. No one did. I took my seat, watched while juror twelve took hers.

She gave the first row a wide berth, avoiding juror four. It was not hard to see why. Ron looked creepy. Why he'd been chosen for the jury was hard to fathom. Even if there was no reason to challenge him for cause, I couldn't imagine a defense attorney or an ADA not exercising a preemptory. Maybe they just lay back, waiting for the other to act, not wanting to use their challenges up, and before they knew what was happening he was seated. Ron looked like hitting on jury chicks was part of his basic MO, which was to hit on anything that moved. If Jeannie Atkins was attractive, there was no way he didn't know her.

My law clerk confidante slid into the seat next to me.

"Hey, dumb dumb," she said. "Wrong juror."

"What?"

"I gave you a lead and who do you talk to? Some bimbo. Jeannie wasn't into women. Wouldn't give them the time of day. I told you, talk to the guys. So do you talk to them? No. You talk to juror twelve, who's got nothing to do with anything."

"She still might know something."

"Not that's going to help you. You want to learn about Jeannie, talk to the people who knew her. Trust me. That's the guys. The juror you're talking to had nothing to do with anything."

Great. That was all I needed. A jealous law clerk who didn't want me sharing my sleuthing activities with anyone else. Who wanted me to investigate the people *she* thought were important.

I felt a tinge of shame. I'd taken solace in coming across someone I actually could feel superior to.

Well, an idea doesn't have to hit me on the head. The law clerk said talk to the guys on the jury. Juror twelve said talk to Ron.

I figured I should talk to Ron.

28

He was sleazier than I thought. And I was thinking sleazy.

"That was one hot broad," he said, with a knowing, macho leer, inviting me into his secret world, just two ass men together.

Much as I appreciated the compliment, I deplored the form in which it came. Juror four not only hit on anything that moved, he bragged about it to anyone willing to listen. I was but not for the reason he thought.

"She was into you in particular?"

"I'll say. Hot to trot, that one was. I barely had to flash her a smile."

That was surely a good thing. Ron's smile would have sent most girls running for the exits.

"Where'd you hook up with her?"

He frowned. "What do you mean?"

"Well, you didn't do her in the jury room, did you? Meet her after court?"

"Why do you ask?"

I smiled. "I'm an old dog, but I like to learn new tricks."

"Oh," he said. "I didn't get to hang out with her that much because she wasn't on the jury. She'd make excuses to be in there, but she wasn't one of us."

"Oh," I said. "Not like she was a juror.'"

"Right."

"Some nice-looking women on that jury."

"I'll say. Like Vicky."

"Vicky?"

"Yeah. Juror twelve."

"Oh, yeah," I said. "She's a dish."

"I'll say. And talk about hot to trot."

"She came on to you too?"

"Well, not like Jeannie. Boy, if the roles were reversed, you know?"

"What do you mean?"

"If Vicky was the law clerk, and Jeannie was on the jury, that would have been just grand." He shook his head. "I can't believe she's gone. What a loss."

"So, what'd you talk to her about? Besides, you know."

"Jeannie? We talked about lunch. Lotta suggestive things about food. Remember that scene in *Tom Jones*?"

Good lord. The man actually saw a film without a car chase. Probably on Turner Classic Movies. I'm amazed he found the channel.

"She ever bring messages from the judge?"

"That's the court officer."

"Right. And the juror—what's her name—Vicky? What did Jeannie think of her?"

"Oh, you know. Two women, one man. They're never happy."

"Jealousy thing."

"That's one way to look at it."

"What's another way?"

"Threesome."

"You're shitting me."

"Hey, I can dream, can't I? But they weren't hostile. They weren't friends, but they weren't hostile."

"That's the only woman on the jury you were interested in?"

"That's the pretty one. Juror five's okay but not in her league. Of course, I'm sitting next to her, wouldn't you know. Juror five, I mean. But you wanna know who's hot?"

"Who's that?"

"The lady lawyer. Whoa! I'd like to have her come in and read some testimony back."

"They don't do that."

"No. The court reporter reads it, and they do it in open court."

I was walking the guy out. When court adjourned, I struck up a conversation by the elevator bank. I followed the avid ass man into the elevator, where the presence of others had not inhibited him from bragging of his exploits, and we were now wending our way down Center Street toward the subway at Chambers. I wasn't sure I wanted to get on the subway with Ron. Neither of us had mentioned where we were going; he had just turned in that direction and I'd tagged along, but as long as he was forthcoming with the information, I was willing to give it a shot.

I never got the chance.

Just as we were passing the massive steps and pillars of the Supreme Court, I was suddenly grabbed from behind and jerked off my feet. My left arm was twisted up behind my back, and before I knew what was happening, I was doubled up over the hood of a parked car.

I managed to twist my head sideways in time to see my quarry hightailing it down the street and get a glimpse of my assailant.

Sergeant Thurman.

128

29

"What the fuck do you think you're doing?"

I was hard-pressed to answer as my face was still pressed up against the car's hood. I managed to croak out, "I'm trying to mate with an Austin-Healey."

Apparently that wasn't the right answer. Thurman jerked me upright, cocked his fist.

I put up my hands. "Whoa! Time out! Tell me what this is all about, and maybe I can answer your questions."

"As if you didn't know," Thurman snarled.

I hate that saying. It's one of Thurman's favorites, and it drives me crazy. If I didn't know, I wouldn't be asking. But I knew from experience that telling him that would only piss him off. "Is there a problem with the case?"

"Why would there be a problem with the case? Have you done anything to fuck it up?"

"No."

He slammed me back down on the car. "Think again."

I thought again. Couldn't come up with a better answer. Decided to keep my mouth shut.

Bad decision. He shook me till I rattled and said, "Any time now."

"If you won't tell me, I'll assume I've done nothing and I'm walking away."

"You're just full of wrong answers," Thurman said. "I'll tell you want you've done. You're messing around in my case. And what happens next? You start talking to the goddamn jurors."

So that was it. How'd he find out so fast? I wondered if my confidante had sold me out. I couldn't see her trading in a private eye for a cop. Particularly *that* cop. But there are a lot of things I don't see. At least, according to Alice.

"You've got to be kidding," I said.

"Oh, yeah? Who were you walking with? Your fucking nephew?"

"Please, Thurman, I'm not that old."

He slammed me against the car again. This time against the door. I was making progress. I managed to stay upright.

I'd had enough.

I wheeled around as fast as I could, managed to break his grip, and got right up in his face. "What do you think I'm doing, you dumb fuck? I came into your office and told you what I knew. Where'd you think I got that? You think I pulled it out of my ass? I nose around, I find out what's going on, I report back to you. You wanna stop me from doing that, I got nothing to report. I was getting something when you fucked it up. Not that I'm apt to get anything now that you scared the shit out of him."

Thurman blinked twice. Tried to adjust to the fact I wasn't quaking in fear. "What the hell are you talking about?"

"I'm trying to separate the wheat from the chaff. You know that expression? The point is, Jeannie Atkins was involved with a lot of people. You wouldn't think the jurors were important, but she happened to be more than usually interested in them. I'm trying to find out why. You don't want to let me, so now you can do it. That juror's name is Ron. He's juror number four. Good luck with that. He may be a little leery of a pushy policeman, but that's not my problem."

Thurman actually took a step backward. "Hey, hey, hey. Why you gettin' so huffy?"

Victory. I had done the impossible. Sergeant Thurman was trying to mollify *me*.

I was on a hot streak. I should try to win the World Series of Poker.

Or walk on water.

30

"I yelled at Thurman."

Alice stared at me. "Are you kidding?"

"I couldn't help it. He had it coming."

"What did he do?"

"He tried to throw me into a car engine. Without opening the hood."

"What?"

"He almost did it too. I wouldn't have thought it was possible. Apparently, it has to do with the amount of thrust."

"So you yelled at him?"

"What'd you expect me to do, congratulate him?"

"You yell at Thurman, he'll beat you up."

"He *was* beating me up. So I yelled."

"What did you say?"

"I said he was blowing the case."

"Great."

"I also called him an asshole and told him to go fuck himself."

"Though not in those words."

"In exactly those words."

"Stanley."

"I was on a roll."

"What the hell are you talking about?"

I gave Alice a rundown of the situation, without dwelling on the attributes of juror twelve.

"You were questioning juror four?"

"Everyone seemed to want me to. Well, except Thurman. At least at the time. What he wants now is open to interpretation."

"So you didn't get anything."

Kill me now.

I thought I had done fairly well. As usual, Alice's assessment of the situation brought me back to Earth.

"I got a lot of leads, a lot of negatives. I got Thurman to lay off and let me do my thing. You want to call that nothing, I suppose that's one way to look at it."

Alice smiled. "Don't take offense. Most detective work is unproductive. You stake out all day long and nothing happens. No one blames you for it."

You could have fooled me. Alice has a way of implying blame with just an inflection. She would tell you that's just how I hear it, but that's how I hear it.

"So, what do you do now?" Alice said, cutting through the bullshit and getting to the gist of the situation.

"I go back to court, try to repair the damage Thurman did, see if I can mend the fence with juror four."

"That seems like a fruitless endeavor."

"You just said most detective work doesn't pay off."

"That doesn't mean you keep doing it."

"And it's not like I got nothing. Jeannie was abnormally interested in the jurors. I'm trying to find out who and why."

"How's it going?"

Is the desire to strangle your wife a universal impulse? I choked down my indignant response, said as calmly as possible, "What would you suggest I do?"

"Get help."

"What?"

"You're obviously not equipped to handle the situation. Richard's in trouble, serious trouble, you're counting on yourself to get him out. Nothing is working, and for all the good relationship–bad relationship you're having with Sergeant Thurman, the bottom line is he thinks Richard did it. And if you talked to him, you'd find out so does the ADA."

"How do you know that?"

"Can you imagine Sergeant Thurman having a theory *contradicting* the ADA? His head would explode. This crap with the jurors is all well and good, but it doesn't look very promising. Why'd you wash out juror twelve?"

"She didn't know Jeannie."

"Who told you that?"

"She did."

"And you believed her? Tell me, does she have big tits?"

"Alice."

"She's wearing something low-cut, and she leans over earnestly to tell you she didn't know her? Well, that settles it. How could she possibly be lying?"

"Her top wasn't low cut."

Alice rolled her eyes. "See? Totally unobservant, couldn't describe what anyone was wearing, but could you see her breasts? *That*, you know."

There was no way I was getting out of the conversation unscathed. It was just a question of what form the scathing took.

"You were gonna tell me what I should be doing. So far you've only told me what I shouldn't."

"I thought I did."

"Did what?"

"Told you what you should be doing."

"I must have missed that tidbit, Alice. Somewhere in the pummeling."

"You're not equipped to put Richard's fate in your hands. You need help."

"You think I should hire a PI?"

"Don't be dumb. *You're* a PI. You may not be the top of your field, but I can't see anyone doing any better."

"Was that a left-handed compliment? Wait, let me get a voice recorder."

"You really wanna screw around? We're talking about Richard."

"I'm not following you, Alice. You say I need help, I say I'll get help, you say why bother, it won't help. What am I missing?"

"You don't need a PI. You need a cop."

31

MacAullif was on the phone when I walked in. He finished his conversation, hung up, and said, "What kept you?"

I blinked. "What?"

"Your buddy's in trouble. I expected you days ago."

"I was *here* days ago. You threw me out."

"Like that's ever stopped you before."

"You should marry my wife."

"I think there's laws about that."

"You said you couldn't help me with the case because Thurman's involved."

"*Nothing* can help you with the case when Thurman's involved. You gotta understand that from the beginning. I do. Thurman's on the case, I give it a wide berth."

I sighed and sank into a chair. "Go ahead, have your fun. Alice beat me up all day, you might as well beat me up all night."

"That sounded gay."

"Really? Then I would say you're oversensitive on the subject."

"You come in here to piss me off or you want help?"

"I want help. I desperately want help. You told me I couldn't have any. I didn't realize that meant I could. I've been wrong about a lot of things lately. You wanna stop fucking around and help me, I'd really appreciate it. It looks like Richard's in some deep shit."

"That's what I hear."

"From whom?"

"Everybody. Cops, ADAs, you name it. The case against Richard is bad. The only reason he hasn't been charged is because he's a pain-in-the-ass shyster and they don't wanna cope with the subsequent shit. You know his prints are on the knife?"

"No, but hum a few bars and I'll fake it."

"That joke kind of dates you. Aside from making you an insensitive asshole."

"Are his prints really on the knife?"

"Yeah."

"And the ADA doesn't think *that's* enough?"

"You don't know Richard's reputation."

"I *work* for him."

"Right. You have an entirely different view. You know he's good. You don't know how he's feared."

"I know no one wants to take him on in a negligence case."

"No one wants to take him on, period. He's gotten you out of a few scrapes, if you'll recall. He didn't do that by smiling and making nice."

"You're saying they're out to get him."

"Only if they *can*. They don't like to lose. It goes on their record. Wins and losses. Just like a pitcher. Only there's no earned run average. And no saves either. Just blown saves. And some losses are worse than others. You blow a slam dunk, people remember."

"You're mixing metaphors."

"You want my help or not?"

"I want your help. I didn't think I'd get it."

MacAullif shrugged. "You're a manic depressive. Tell me about the girl with tits."

My mouth fell open. "Did Alice call you?"

"Why?"

"How'd you know about the girl with tits?"

"There's always a girl with tits. She may not have anything to do with the case, but you manage to make her important."

"I don't do that."

"So, from your question about Alice I can assume there is a girl with tits and your wife already knows about her. What's the story?"

I told him about juror twelve.

MacAullif rolled his eyes. "Oh, my god. An enigmatic clue and a pair of tits. No wonder the rest of the case has paled into insignificance."

"I don't think cops are allowed to say *enigmatic*."

"The number twelve is a long shot at best. Particularly if she denies knowing the decedent. Though your professional opinion she was telling the truth increases the chance she was lying."

"So, what would you do about her?"

"Try to get her shirt off. I should probably talk to her."

"Ah. That's why you asked if there were any tits involved."

"Not at all. That was just good investigative technique. Thurman really tried to push you through a car?"

"His heart wasn't in it. You've done it harder."

"That also sounded gay."

"You're really homophobic today. That, coupled with an insistence that you're interested in breasts, suggests you're halfway out of the closet."

MacAullif shook his head. "You know, talking to you used to be a lot more fun."

"I'm old, I'm tired, I can't keep up. Can you help Richard or not?"

"I don't know. It's not looking good. The evidence is mounting up and there are no other suspects."

"What about juror twelve?"

"What about her? According to you, she didn't know shit."

"What about the lady lawyer and the ADA?"

"What about 'em?"

"If you got a love triangle with Jeannie Atkins, the ADA, and the lady lawyer, it could add up. Jeannie Atkins and the ADA are hot and heavy. The lady lawyer comes between 'em. Jeannie Atkins doesn't take it well. She threatens to tell the judge. That would not be just a juicy scandal, it could be the end of their careers. One or the other of them takes action."

"One or the other?"

"I don't wanna be a sexist pig and say the girl couldn't have done it."

"Give me a break," MacAullif said. "The point is the ADA is the one risking his job. The lady lawyer could be just going the extra mile for her client."

"You don't mean that."

"Sure, I do. Who's on shakier ethical ground? The guy from the DA's office or the hotshot attorney racking up the billable hours? Anyway, if you're pushing that scenario, I bet on the ADA."

"You think I'm right?"

"It would be a first, but it's not a deal breaker. I just don't like it much."

"Why not?"

"Fucking the lawyer costs you your job. Killing the law clerk sends you to jail."

"If you're caught."

"Yeah, yeah, yeah, risk, reward, probability, yada yada yada. I'm not ruling it out, but I don't like it."

"What *do* you like?"

"I like cigars. My doctor won't let me smoke 'em."

"Who do you like for the crime?"

"I have no idea. I haven't investigated it."

"You going to?"

"No. That's not the type of help you need."

"What do you mean?"

"You're not going to get Richard off by finding the 'real killer.' You're going to get him off the old-fashioned, O. J. Simpson way, with a verdict of not guilty. I can help prepare you for that."

"He's not even arrested."

"That's a technicality. His prints are on the knife."

"Why haven't we heard about that? I would think the prosecutor would be shouting it from the rooftops."

"If he wanted to charge him. He's still getting his ducks in a row. Meanwhile he's playing 'em close to the vest."

"Anything else he's withholding?"

"Probably. But he's also withholding it from me."

"Why?"

"Because he thinks I'd tell you."

"How'd you find out about the prints?"

"I have my sources."

"Your sources got anything else?"

"I'll check 'em out."

"You haven't checked 'em out?"

"This wasn't a high priority. You hadn't even asked."

I didn't see any use pointing out again that I was in there days ago. I got up to go.

"I get anything, you want me to call you on your cell?" MacAullif said.

"Beep me. I'll call you."

He shook his head. "Still usin' a pager? You know the drug dealers have moved on to cell phones."

"They make more than I do."

32

It didn't make the front page of the next day's *New York Post*. If Richard had been even the least supporting actor on a TV show, instead of the best negligence lawyer in the world, he would have had Page One wrapped up. The story had everything: sex, betrayal, murder. Though I think the betrayal part was a stretch. I don't think the ADA was clear on the motive. The case just finally reached the point where he had to pull the trigger.

Nonetheless, the story got plenty of play. There was a shot of Richard being hauled out of his office in handcuffs—someone must have tipped the press—plus a glamour shot of the victim. A splatter shot of the corpse no doubt would have bumped the story up to a two-page spread. Even without it, Richard rated a teaser box on the front page: "Client Killer, page 5."

That was hardly fair. Jeannie wasn't Richard's client. Apparently the paper figured Richard wouldn't make a big stink about being charged with killing his girlfriend, not his client.

But I didn't even know about the arrest at that point. I was in court, trying to mend fences Sergeant Thurman had steamrolled over.

Ron was a tough sell. Not that I could blame him. You see Sergeant Thurman beating on some poor schmuck, it's hard to wanna step up and say, "Next." I tried to reassure him. Thurman was an old pal. This was a routine ritual we went through every time we met, things were cool or why would I be back in court?

If Ron believed me, you wouldn't have known it. He nodded and smiled and kept his distance.

Meanwhile, the ADA and the attractive defense attorney were acting out *West Side Story*. I'm probably just projecting, but I could have sworn the other defense attorneys were getting a little miffed at the cute lady lawyer who was taking it easy on the prosecution's witnesses. I figured they suspected the liaison: "A boy like that would prosecute your brother . . . A boy who prosecutes cannot love."

Anyway, in the midst of all that nonsense, I noticed an undercurrent among the other attorneys, a low, excited buzz out of keeping with the normal courtroom decorum.

During the first recess I grabbed my confidante. "What's going on?"

"They arrested him."

"Who?"

"Your buddy."

"When?"

"Just now."

I pushed my way to the door to the judge's chambers.

The bailiff headed me off. "You can't go in there."

"No, but you can. Tell the judge I gotta see him."

"You don't summon the judge. He summons you."

"I know."

He stared me down. Seemed to be calculating how much of a pain in the ass it would be to have me physically removed from the premises. He must have decided it wasn't worth it.

"Wait here."

He was back in a minute and ushered me into chambers.

The judge was having a muffin. I wondered if he ate on every break.

He cocked his head and said, "I assume this is about Richard Rosenberg."

"Has he been arrested?"

"He has."

"Why?"

"They say he killed his girlfriend."

"Yeah, yeah, yeah," I said impatiently. "They didn't think they had enough evidence. What makes them think they do now?"

"Apparently they found more."

"Apparently?"

"I have my own case. I don't keep up with theirs."

"You knew he was arrested."

"Everyone knows that."

"When did it happen?"

He shrugged. "Maybe an hour ago."

I bolted out of the judge's chambers, waited impatiently for the elevator, went down to the lockup.

Richard wasn't there.

Thurman was.

"You arrested Richard?"

"That's a surprise?"

"You didn't tell me you were going to do it."

"I'm sorry. Should I have checked with you first?"

"Where is he?"

"Probably back in his office. They tried to hold him, but apparently the guy knows some law."

I turned on my heel and walked out.

"Don't stop feeding me stuff," Thurman yelled after me.

33

Wendy and Janet were buzzing like bees. I'd never seen them so excited. I'd rarely seen them together. Usually, one was sufficient to run the desk. Either Richard was pulling out all the stops or whoever was on the desk called the other and she couldn't stay home.

They turned on me when I came in.

"I thought you were protecting him," Wendy accused.

That seemed harsh. I had to make allowances for her being upset. "I just found out. You should have beeped me."

"I *did* beep you," Janet said. "You didn't answer."

Of course. I'd turned my pager off for court and never turned it back on. "How is he?"

"He isn't happy," Janet said. In her case I didn't know if the colossal understatement was intended as such or if she was being serious.

"Anyone in there?"

"No."

I started for the door.

"Let me tell him you're here," Wendy said. At least I think it was Wendy. My back was to them, and I can't tell their voices apart even when they're not on the phone.

Richard was at his desk going over files.

"What are you doing?" I said.

"Checking the cases." He gestured to them. "You've been bringing me shit."

"I always bring you shit. You reject ninety percent of the cases I sign. It's not like I go out and find them for you. I sign the clients Wendy and Janet give me."

"You should reject some of them."

"You'd fire me for it. And you'd crab about paying. Why should you pay for sign-ups I didn't sign?"

Richard started flare up, then shook his head. "True. Where have you been?"

"Sitting in court."

"You charging me for that?"

"Only if I do you any good."

"You mean you are?"

"Why do you say that?"

"You wouldn't offer to work for nothing unless you thought it was a moot point."

"Richard, I got leads. They don't mean much in light of you getting arrested. Do you know what they've got on you?"

"No, I don't. I'm charged with murder."

"You're out on bail?"

"I'm out on my own recognizance."

"How'd that happen?"

"ADA didn't want a bail hearing. Figured he'd get creamed and I'd get information."

"So how you gonna handle the case?"

"Brilliantly and with amazing savoir faire."

"Richard."

"I don't know how I'm going to handle the case because I don't know what the case is. As I find out, I will develop a defense strategy. I assure you it will be original, ingenious, and spectacular."

"How about effective?"

"That goes without saying. If only I can find out what the ADA's got."

"Well, your prints are on the knife."

Richard's face froze. "What!"

"The murder weapon. Your prints are on it."

"Are you sure?"

"Yeah."

"Where'd you get that?"

"MacAullif."

"You didn't think it was important enough to pass along?"

"I just got it."

"This morning?"

"Last night."

"How the hell did my prints get on the knife?"

"Do you even know what knife they're talking about?"

"They said a knife from the kitchen."

"That's a lot of latitude. Did you ever touch a knife in her apartment?"

"Ah—oh, my god!"

"What?"

"We ordered takeout. Sometimes it's Chinese, sometimes it's Mexican, sometimes it's Thai. Sometimes it's something that needs to be cut."

"Shit."

"MacAullif have pictures of the prints?"

"Not that I know of."

"Could he get one?"

"I don't know. He says the cops are shutting him out."

Richard nodded grimly. "Yeah. They must have closed ranks when they decided to charge me. That's one thing you can do. See if MacAullif can get a picture. They'll have to show me in court, but I'd rather have it going in."

"You gonna demand a probable cause hearing?"

"I'm going to waive it."

"What!"

"I'm going to waive probable cause, demand they go right to trial."

"Why?"

"Get this over with."

"Yeah, but you wanna win."

"I'm gonna win."

"Richard, you wanna know what the prosecutor's got. You find things out at a probable cause hearing. That's why lawyers insist on them."

"You find *some* things out at a probable cause hearing. Like the Milton Berle story."

"What Milton Berle story?"

"You never heard that? Well, it's not one they ever told on the Carson show. Milton Berle had a huge cock. Everybody knew it. So when this drunken millionaire gambler starts bragging how well hung he is, a bunch of Vegas sharks bet him a ton of money it's not as big as Miltie's. Only Uncle Miltie don't wanna play. They plead with him: he doesn't have to put up any money, all he's gotta do is show his cock. Finally, Miltie throws up his hands. 'Okay,' he says, 'I'll do it. But I'm only going to show enough to win.'"

Richard shrugged. "That's how it is at a probable cause hearing. ADA's only gonna show enough to win."

"So?"

"I want the full Miltie."

34

"*People versus Richard Rosenberg.*"

"Scott Drexler for the prosecution."

"Richard Rosenberg for the defense."

Judge Hollins leaned down from the bench. A no-nonsense young judge, he already had a reputation for keeping lawyers in line. "You're serving as your own attorney?"

"You knew that, Your Honor."

"I want it in the record. You are serving as your own attorney?"

"I am."

"You know what they say about a lawyer who conducts his own defense?"

"He has a fool for a client, Your Honor. But I believe that fool is within his rights."

Judge Hollins seemed somewhat taken aback by that rejoinder. "Just so we have no illusions." He turned to the court bailiff. "Call the first jurors."

Jury selection for a criminal case, particularly for a murder, is a long and complicated process somewhat akin to Doctor House's replacing his staff at the beginning of season four. You may recall he hired forty doctors for the three positions and slowly winnowed it down over the course of the season by firing thirty-seven of them. In this case they called fifty jurors, which wouldn't be nearly enough. They needed to seat sixteen, twelve jurors and four alternates.

The first fifty candidates were paraded into the courtroom, sat in the spectators' seats. I was in the spectators' seats myself, in the first row right behind the defense table. As the jurors filed in, I met Richard at the rail.

"How long do you expect jury selection to take?"

Richard shrugged. "I don't know this ADA."

"How long are you going to take?"

"Not very."

"I'll have time to check out the other trial?"

"You'll have time to get a law degree."

The court officer took the jurors' ballots up to the front of courtroom, placed them in a metal drum, gave it a spin, and began drawing them out one at a time and reading off each juror's name. The ballots were the little squares of paper that had summoned them for jury duty in the first place and followed them everywhere they went. Throughout the course of their jury selection experience, the jurors were constantly handing their ballots in or picking their ballots up.

As each juror's name was called, he or she would come up and be seated in the jury box. Their ballot would then be placed in a slot in a board that corresponded to the number of their seat. The board was for the lawyers to refer to in order to address them by name during voire dire, the questioning of the prospective jurors.

Once the first sixteen jurors had been seated, Richard stood up, glanced at the board, and approached the jury.

He smiled at juror four. "Mr. Fuller. Do you think you can be fair?"

Mr. Fuller was somewhat startled by the direct question. He hesitated a moment, smiled, and said, "I think so."

"Thank you," Richard said. He raised his eyes. "How about the rest of you? Do you think you can be fair?"

The jurors looked around at each other. Of course no one blurted out an answer.

"Well, let me put it this way," Richard said. "Is there anyone who thinks they *can't* be fair? Please. Speak up or raise your hand."

No one did.

"Fine." Richard turned to the judge. "Jury's acceptable," he said. He set the board on the prosecution table and went and sat down.

That produced a rumbling in the court. There were no spectators except the rest of the fifty jurors, who were watching the voire dire to see what they might expect. None expected that. Many began talking.

The ADA was severely discombobulated. He had a whispered conversation with his second chair.

"Mr. Drexler," Judge Hollins prompted.

Drexler, in midconversation, raised his hand. "One moment, Your Honor." After one last whisper he picked up the board, approached the jury box, and began a painstaking interrogation of the jurors.

After the first two or three questions Richard turned around in his chair, smiled, and waved his fingers at me in a dismissive, fly-away-little-bird gesture.

I got up and slipped out of the courtroom.

I bet the jurors wished they could have.

I looked in on the Global Bank trial. That it was still going on was not surprising. That they had enough jurors left to do it was something of a miracle.

They hadn't seemed to have made much progress, except for the deepening looks of despair on the faces of the jurors.

My confidante sidled up to me during recess. "Thought you'd abandoned us."

"Got another trial."

"So I hear. Juicy murder case. What I wouldn't give to be in that court."

"Not today, you wouldn't."

"Oh?"

"Jury selection."

"I thought your Rosenberg was entertaining."

"He was. In the traditional showbiz way."

"What's that?"

"Leave 'em wanting more."

I described Richard's voire dire interrogation. My confidante was amused. I'd forgotten her name. Didn't know how to ask it. I could ask the other law clerk, but I didn't know his name either. I wondered if it was on record somewhere.

She said, "Let me know if anything happens."

"Why?"

"Are you kidding me? Here, *nothing* happens. I'm desperate for a tidbit."

She batted her eyes at me as if she might be desperate for something else. That was a complication that hadn't occurred to me. I wondered if it was because she wasn't particularly attractive or because I was getting too old to have thought of it. Whatever the reason, she tempted me not. But I was shamelessly willing to exploit anything.

"With Jeannie gone, you have to deal with the jurors more than you used to, right?"

152

"Yeah, why?"

"Ron clammed up on me. You think you could sound him out? I'd kind of like to pump the guy for info, and the well dried up."

"I'll give it a shot," she said.

She winked at me.

Uh oh.

Wait'll I tell Alice about this.

35

Even with Richard's accepting every juror that came into the box, jury selection took three days. The only purpose his tactic had served was to create the impression the defense was reasonable and open, had nothing to hide, and was perfectly happy with the jury, while the prosecutor was mean and suspicious and thought they all were filthy lying scum.

The ADA's opening statement didn't help. He kept insisting on the point that if he proved his case beyond a reasonable doubt, they were legally compelled to bring in a verdict of guilty whether they wanted to or not, and they damn well better do it. In light of his didactic insistence, his presentation of the facts was skimpy at best.

In contrast, Richard's opening statement was short, sweet, and casual. Just because the prosecutor said something didn't make it true; the jurors could do anything they wanted, they should listen to the evidence and decide for themselves, not because either of the lawyers told them what to do. The end result was that by the time the prosecutor started calling witnesses, Richard had twelve friends on the jury—sixteen, counting the alternates.

36

ADA Scott Drexler led off with the super, who testified to going into Jeannie Atkins's apartment with a passkey and finding the body.

"And what time was that?" Drexler said.

"It was around eleven o'clock in the morning."

"Why did you enter her apartment?"

"I got a phone call saying Jeannie Atkins was supposed to be in court, had not arrived, and was not answering her phone. The judge said this was unusual and I should check on her."

"Where did you find her?"

"She was lying on her bed."

"What was her condition?"

"She was clearly dead. She'd been stabbed by a knife. Several times. The body'd been hacked up pretty badly. There was blood all over the sheets."

"How was the decedent dressed?"

"She was nude."

"Where were the wounds?"

"In her chest. Her breasts had been slashed, and she looked like she'd been stabbed in the heart."

"What did you do?"

"I left everything exactly as it was and called the police."

"From what phone?"

"From my cell phone."

"So you didn't touch anything in the apartment?"

"No, I did not."

"Thank you. That's all."

"Mr. Rosenberg?" Judge Hollins said.

I was looking forward to seeing Richard rip the super's can off, but he declined to cross-examine.

There followed a procession of cops, detectives, and medics from the Emergency Medical Service unit, all of whom testified to arriving at the crime scene and finding the decedent. All observed that she was lying in bed covered in blood. All noticed she was nude.

Richard didn't cross-examine any of them, which seemed a good move. No new information was being imparted, and there was no reason to dwell on the gore.

The medical examiner's testimony led to the first real bone of contention. Dr. Nash was an important witness, and he knew it. A rather prissy man with a snooty air, he radiated contempt for the lowlifes who perpetrated such heinous crimes and gloried in the fact that his expertise would be instrumental in putting the defendant away.

The smug way he rattled off his qualifications set my teeth on edge.

I couldn't wait for Richard to get a crack at him.

Instead Richard stipulated to his qualifications without asking a single question.

Dr. Nash testified to arriving at the scene, pronouncing Jeannie Atkins dead, and sending the body to the morgue for autopsy.

"And when did you perform your autopsy?" ADA Drexler asked.

"Within a half hour from the time I pronounced her dead at the scene. The EMS units are good. In a situation like that they don't waste time."

"And when you performed your autopsy, what did you find?"

"My autopsy confirmed what I had observed at the crime scene. The victim was killed by multiple stab wounds to the chest. One of the wounds had penetrated the heart. That wound in itself was sufficient to have caused death. The other wounds were certainly contributing factors, but the knife wound to the heart was decisive."

"Are you saying the woman wouldn't have died if she hadn't been stabbed in the heart?"

"I'm not saying that at all. The other wounds alone were probably sufficient to have caused death. The wound to the heart definitely was. The wound had severed the aorta. The victim simply could not have lived."

I was watching the jurors' faces during this, and my heart sank. The sympathetic look Richard had instilled on their faces was gone. Their jaws were set. Their eyes were hard. This was murder. This was ugly. Someone had to pay.

ADA Drexler returned to the prosecution table, consulted his notes, giving the jurors a little time dwell on the horror. He closed his notes, turned back to the witness stand. "And did you determine the time of death, Doctor?"

"Yes, I did."

"And what time was that?"

"Death occurred sometime between eleven o'clock and one A.M."

"Thank you, Doctor. That's all."

"Mr. Rosenberg. Any questions?"

Richard hesitated just long enough to let the doctor think he might get off the stand. "I have one or two questions."

I could see the jurors' interest perk up. This was the first witness Richard had deigned to cross-examine. Clearly, this was important. Some jurors were even leaning forward so as not to miss what he was about to say.

Richard stood and approached the witness.

The doctor bristled. From the clipped, decisive tones with which he had snapped out his answers to the ADA, he gave the impression of a man who was not used to having his word challenged. He knew what he knew, and no damn shyster was going to say any different.

"Eleven to one, doctor?"

"That's right."

"That's a rather wide window of opportunity, isn't it?"

"It takes into account every possibility."

Richard's eyebrows raised. "Ah. Possibility. So these are the *possible* times of death? As opposed to the *likely* times of death?"

"These are perfectly likely times of death," the doctor snapped.

"But some are more likely than others, aren't they, Doctor?"

"That's not what I said."

"I know it's not what you said. I'm asking you if that's the case."

"No, that's not the case."

"Really? You said it was a broad time block to take in all possibilities. One would assume the outer limits are the times you included to allow for any *remote* possibilities."

"That's why it's dangerous to make assumptions."

"You're saying that is not the case?"

"No, absolutely not. Any of those times are likely."

"Eleven to eleven fifteen is just as likely as eleven forty-five to midnight?"

"Neither would surprise me. The time of death is not something you can make book on. The whole idea is offensive."

"Offensive or not, I'm asking you if that is the case."

"The answer is no."

"So. Eleven to one is one is your story and you're sticking to it."

"Objection, Your Honor."

"Sustained."

"Tell me, Doctor. Were those figures in your original report?"

"I beg your pardon?"

"The time of death. Between eleven and one o'clock. When you examined the body, were they in your original report?"

The doctor hesitated. "They were not in my preliminary report. Which was death as a result of stab wound to the heart. But they were certainly in my first final report."

Richard smiled. "Interesting choice of words, Doctor. Your 'first final report.' Talk about an oxymoron! Clearly, neither word is true. It is in neither your first report *nor* your final report."

The doctor shifted uncomfortably on the stand.

"Objection, Your Honor. I don't hear a question."

"Could you put that in the form of a question, Mr. Rosenberg?"

"Sounds like we're on *Jeopardy*, Your Honor."

Some jurors looked startled. Richard was, after all, the defendant.

Judge Hollins banged the gavel. "That will do. It is customary for the judge to make allowances for a defendant serving as his own attorney. However, in this case you *are* an attorney, Mr. Rosenberg. You know what's proper."

"Yes, Your Honor. I *would* like an answer to my *original* question. I asked him if the time of death was in his first report. He just told me it was in his first final report. In light of that nonanswer I'll have to ask a few more questions."

"Proceed."

"When did you issue your first final report?"

"When?"

"Yes. I assume it was before your *last* final report. Or even your *second* final report. Or your *penultimate* final report. But since this is the final report you claim contained the time of death, pray, enlighten us. When did you issue your *first* final report?"

"I really couldn't say."

"You couldn't say?"

"No."

"Is that because you don't know or because you've been instructed not to?"

"Objection, Your Honor."

"Overruled. In light of the doctor's previous answers, it is a legitimate question."

"I was *not* instructed not to say. I resent the implication."

"It wasn't an implication. It was a direct question. With regard to the first part of the question, which you have *not* answered, is it because you don't know?"

"That's right." The doctor said it through clenched lips. "I don't know."

"I thought not, Doctor. So, you are uncertain regarding your testimony as to the time of death?"

ADA Drexler nearly catapulted from his seat. "Your Honor, Your Honor! The witness said no such thing! Counsel's summarizing of his testimony borders on contempt of court!"

"I believe I'm on the right side of the border, Your Honor," Richard said. "I'm trying to interpret the witness's testimony. If I'm wrong, he can correct me."

"You're wrong," the doctor sputtered indignantly. "I *do* know the time of death. With regard to the narrow scope of your question, I don't know *exactly* when I logged it in my report."

"Well, let me put it this way. Was it before the police questioned the doorman and my driver as to when I left the building?"

"Objection," ADA Wexler said. "How could the doctor possibly know that?"

"Well, then, he can say he doesn't know. The witness is very good at saying he doesn't know."

Judge Hollins's gavel cut off ADA Drexler's sputtering objection. "That will do. Attorneys. In my chambers."

37

They were gone half an hour. When they returned, Richard looked complacent, Drexler looked angry, and Judge Hollins looked grim.

"Return the witness to the stand," Judge Hollins said. "Dr. Nash, I remind you that you are still under oath. Mr. Rosenberg, you may resume questioning the witness."

Richard stood, bowed slightly, and stepped up in front of the witness stand. "No further questions," he said and turned around and sat down.

Judge Hollins scowled.

I knew why. No matter what went on in the judge's chambers, even if it was all three of them just ordering a sandwich, Richard had created the impression that he had been read the riot act, and his cross-examination had been curtailed. Considering that he was the defendant, that had to create a great deal of sympathy for him with the jury.

Even more frustrating for the judge, Richard was being so calm, courteous, and polite, there was absolutely nothing to reprimand him for. And even if there was, Judge Hollins was not going to do it in front of the jury, and if he had called the attorneys back into chambers when absolutely nothing had happened and Richard certainly hadn't done anything to warrant it, it would be even worse.

Judge Hollins turned to the prosecutor. "Any redirect, Mr. Drexler?"

Drexler took a breath. "I have one or two more questions."

Richard grinned. "Apparently I didn't ask the right questions on cross-examination."

Judge Hollins banged the gavel. "That will do. Mr. Rosenberg, I'm trying to give you leeway, but you know what's proper. Do not make me find you in contempt of court."

"Sorry, Your Honor. I'll be quiet," Richard said. He hunched over slightly at the defendant's table, playing on the image of the little man beaten into submission by the powerful judge.

I realized he had made his remark expressly for that purpose.

Drexler approached the witness stand. "You testified, Doctor, the time of death was between eleven and one?"

"That's right."

"On what factors do you base that conclusion?"

"Body temperature, for one thing."

"Would you explain that to the jurors?"

"Certainly. As you all know, during life the body temperature is ninety-eight point six. Upon death, the body cools. The rate of cooling is a constant. The body cools at a rate of approximately one-half degree Fahrenheit per hour. I took the body temperature at eleven o'clock in the morning. At that time the body temperature was ninety-three point three. So the body had cooled five point three degrees. Five degrees would indicate the body had cooled for ten hours. Which would put the time of death around one o'clock. But we have more than that. We have three-tenths of a degree, more than half of the five-tenths of a degree that would indicate another hour. Which places the median time of death at approximately midnight. One hour either way gives us a true bracket of the time of death."

Drexler nodded approvingly. "Thank you, Doctor. You said that's one way. Are there others?"

"Oh, yes. The examination of the stomach contents can tell you when the decedent met her death relative to the time she ingested her last meal."

"And in this case?"

"The decedent died approximately three hours after eating steak, potatoes, and spinach. She also had cognac."

"Thank you, Doctor. That's all."

Richard rose, smiled at the witness. "Doctor, you're rather eager to slant your testimony in the favor of the prosecution, aren't you?"

"Most certainly not," he snapped. "I am testifying to the facts."

"You are testifying to your conclusions based on your examination of the body, are you not?"

"That's right."

"And your conclusions are colored by a desire to help the prosecution, are they not?"

"I resent that!"

"Resent it all you like, Doctor, but please answer it."

"My medical findings are slanted in no way to help the prosecution."

"Really? Well, Doctor, you were scrupulously careful to avoid testifying to any hearsay, but I think we're all aware that the prosecution has witnesses to show I was in that apartment on the night of the murder and left sometime before midnight."

"Objection. Hearsay."

Richard cocked his head. "You object to my admitting I was in the apartment?"

Once again the gavel came down. "*I* object to it," Judge Hollins said. "You are not giving testimony or making a speech. If you have a point to make, please do so by legal means."

"Yes, Your Honor. Doctor, I am asking you, *in your own mind*, when you calculated the time of death, were you aware that the police had evidence I was in that apartment and left before midnight?"

"Objection."

"Overruled. The question as it is now framed relates only to what the witness was thinking. I'll allow it."

"I may have heard something to that effect."

"And when you picked midnight as the median time death might have occurred, instead of twelve thirty, which is actually closer, were you slanting your findings to help the prosecution?"

"Objection. Already asked and answered."

"Sustained."

"Well, let's examine your findings, Doctor. The body temperature at eleven o'clock in the morning was ninety-three point three. The body has cooled five and three-tenths degrees. You're saying five degrees is ten hours and three-tenths is another hour. Wouldn't *five*-tenths be an hour, doctor?"

"That's an approximation."

"Oh, that's an approximation. Then let's examine that approximation, Doctor. Ninety-three point one degrees would be eleven hours, would it not? So, ninety-three point three degrees would be ten hours and thirty-six minutes. Tell me, Doctor, is ten hours and thirty-six minutes closer to eleven hours or ten hours and a half?"

"That's absurd."

"Absurd? It's your math."

The doctor said nothing, and glowered on the stand.

"Well, let's look at your other time of death, Doctor. Excuse me. I don't mean your other time of death. I mean the other method at which you arrived at your predetermined time of death."

"Objection to the word *predetermined*."

"Sustained. Rephrase your question, Mr. Rosenberg."

"With regard to the stomach contents, isn't it pretty much the same thing?"

"What do you mean?"

"The police told you when she ate her dinner, so you adjusted your findings so as to correspond with the body temperature."

"Objection!" Drexler thundered. "That is a monstrous accusation!"

"I did nothing of the sort!" the doctor snapped.

"The witness has chosen not to wait for a ruling on your objection," Judge Hollins said dryly, "rendering it moot. Doctor, in the future would you attempt to adhere to proper courtroom decorum?"

"Yes, Your Honor."

"Doctor, prior to your calculating the time of death based on the stomach contents, had you been told when the decedent ate her last meal?"

"Objection. Hearsay."

"I'll rephrase. Before you calculated the time of death from the stomach contents, had you, in your own mind, any idea of when the decedent ate her last meal?"

"Objection."

"Overruled."

"Only by hearsay."

"Naturally, Doctor. Only by hearsay. Unless you took the decedent out to dinner. Which you didn't. I took the decedent out to dinner. But in your own mind, when you performed your calculations, did you know when I was alleged to have done that?"

The doctor took a breath. "Yes, I did."

"Well, there's a refreshing burst of candor."

"Mr. Rosenberg."

"Sorry, Your Honor."

"Now, doctor, your autopsy showed the presence of a great deal of blood on the body, did it not?"

"Yes, it did."

"Did you find any other fluids on the body?"

"I beg your pardon?"

"Aside from the blood. For instance, did you find any semen on the body?"

ADA Drexler's mouth fell open. Evidently, he'd expected Richard to fight to keep any mention of semen out.

"Doctor?" Richard prompted.

"Ah, yes, I did."

"You found semen on the body?"

"I found traces on the breasts and traces in the mouth."

"Uh, huh. Indicating some sort of sexual activity shortly before death?"

"Yes. Unless it had been placed there postmortem."

Richard made a face. "That is a repugnant idea, Doctor. Tell me, when you found the semen, did that immediately spring to mind?"

"Objection, Your Honor."

"The doctor used the example. I'd like to know if it was one that occurred to him during his autopsy or something he thought up preparing for cross-examination."

"Nonetheless, the objection to the question in that form is sustained. You may rephrase the question."

"Let's not bother," Richard said. "Doctor, I'm assuming you're not the one who compared the semen to my DNA sample and proved that it's mine. However, conceding that it is, and that I was in the apartment with Jeannie Atkins shortly before she was killed, let me ask you this: Would the presence of semen indicate that the decedent was engaged in some sort of sexual activity shortly before she was killed?"

"Unless it was postmortem."

"Yes, yes, I concede the point, Doctor. But in all likelihood, did that not indicate sexual activity on the part of the victim?"

"Yes, it did."

"Tell me, Doctor, during sex does the pulse rate quicken?"

"That is not my field of expertise."

"Yes, I understand. But it does, doesn't it?"

"Yes, it does."

"The blood pressure rises, does it not?"

"I'm a doctor. I object to being cross-examined on subjects outside the scope of my medical training."

"This is something even a layman would know. You've had sex, haven't you, Doctor?"

"Objection! Of all the inappropriate, rude questions!"

"The doctor said the pulse rate quickens. He must have *some* basis for that assertion."

"The objection is reluctantly overruled."

"Have you ever had sex, Doctor?"

"Yes, I have."

"Was another person involved?"

Drexler was prepared to thunder an objection, but Judge Hollins beat him to it. "Sidebar!" he snapped.

The sidebar was brief. When the attorneys resumed their positions, Richard had a bemused smile on his face.

I wondered how that played with the jury.

"Now, then, Doctor," Richard said. "Granted, this is not your field of study, but can we assume you know a few basic facts regarding sexual acts?"

"You're asking me as a layman?"

"I'm asking you as a doctor. While this is not your field of expertise, you are a learned man and your opinions have weight. I'm sure the jurors understand that this is outside the scope of a medical examiner. In your opinion, the pulse rate quickens during sex?"

"Yes, it does."

"Blood pressure rises?"

"That's right."

"And the temperature rises. Doesn't it?"

The doctor frowned. "I don't believe that's so."

"Really? You've heard the term 'hot and bothered,' haven't you? Or think of two sweaty bodies locked in an embrace. Isn't their temperature elevated? Aren't they warmer than normal?"

"I don't know."

"You don't know?"

"No."

"You know about the pulse rate and the blood pressure. But you don't know about the temperature?"

"I am not certain about the temperature. I don't think it does."

Richard grinned. "Are you really not sure or did you just figure out what I'm getting at?"

"Objection."

"Overruled."

"I'm not sure," the doctor said stubbornly.

"Well, let me put it this way, Doctor. Your calculation as to the time of death is based on the assumption that Jeannie Atkins's body temperature was ninety-eight point six when she died. If it were greater, even by a half a degree, would that throw off your calculations by as much as a whole hour, making it seem as if Jeannie Atkins died a whole hour earlier than she actually did? In which case your time of death would actually be between midnight and two A.M."

"Objection."

"Overruled," Judge Hollins said, and the look on his face was the most encouraging thing I'd seen since the beginning of the trial. The judge was actually considering Richard's premise. Which meant the jurors were too.

Richard Rosenberg, with a seemingly absurd line of questioning, had beaten the doctor to a standstill.

38

Richard invited me back to the office to discuss the case. I would have been flattered, but I knew it wasn't for my expertise. He just wanted a cheerleader to bounce ideas off. Which was fine with me. After watching the trial all day, I couldn't think about anything else.

"So, how do you think it's going?" Richard said.

I smiled. "That's a hell of a question."

"Why?"

"You're putting on the most unconventional defense ever. I have no idea what you're doing, and the ADA doesn't either. You want me to evaluate its effectiveness, I would say you have them completely discombobulated. On the other hand, you stipulated being in the woman's apartment when she was killed, and providing the semen that was on the body."

"And are there any of those things the prosecutor couldn't have proved?" Richard said.

"Probably not."

"Then I fail to see your point. What I've done, Stanley, is stolen his thunder. When the prosecutor starts making these points, the jurors' jaws won't be dropping, because they dropped when I said it. I stole the punch lines, and I get the applause."

"Is that how you see it?"

"I hope it's how the jury does. A trial is a show. You gotta put on a good one."

"Richard, I watched you handle a murder trial before. For your friend, Anson Carbinder. And you didn't pull any of these stunts."

"Of course not. Anson would have freaked out. Who wouldn't, for Christ's sake? Besides, I was at a distinct disadvantage in that case."

"Why?"

"I didn't know if he was guilty."

"So that's your advantage. You know you're not guilty."

"Or I know I am."

"Richard."

"Either way is helpful, Stanley. An attorney is either fumbling in the dark or working toward a predetermined goal. It's not important what that goal is. What's important is knowing it."

"Richard."

"Sorry. Was I in lecture mode again? It's hard to resist, since the judge won't let me use it. The point is, I'm innocent. I'm not going to hang myself out to dry with revelations of things I didn't do. Which is great. I can jump ahead of the prosecutor by stipulating to anything he's going to be able to prove. Which has got to piss him off."

"What's the elevated temperature thing?"

"A bunch of bullshit. But so's the time of death."

"What?"

171

"Come on. Eleven to one? And that asshole has the gall to say eleven is as likely as midnight. You know it isn't, I know it isn't, he knows it isn't, the judge knows it isn't. The jury should know it isn't, but they're the great unwashed—who the fuck knows what they're thinking?"

"Richard."

"The doctor was saying something that wasn't true. But it's not *disprovable*. It's his *opinion*. He's *entitled* to it. The fact he's a quack and his opinion carries weight is a bitter pill to swallow."

"Are you saying he's lying about the time of death?"

"No, I'm saying exactly what I said. He's slanting his figures to help the prosecution, and he's been doing it for so many years he doesn't even know he is. What, he takes the temperature at eleven A.M. and says she died at midnight? And then acts like the number's set in stone? Give me a break."

"So, what can you do about it?"

"Exactly what I'm doing. Ridicule the notion and ask him about his sex life." Richard waved it away. "Today was easy. Basically batting practice. The prosecution lobbing fastballs over the heart of the plate so I could get in some swings. Tomorrow will be different. Tomorrow they start lobbing grenades."

"What happens then?"

"Then I'm fucked."

39

Day two was just like Richard said. They were out to get him. It was all he could do to keep ducking and tap-dancing out of the way. That he got in some counterpunches was much to his credit.

Having established that Jeannie Atkins had indeed been murdered, ADA Drexler proceeded to put Richard at the scene of the crime.

The driver from the car service testified to driving Richard and Jeannie Atkins to dinner, driving them back to her apartment, and waiting outside when they went in.

"And how long was the defendant in Jeannie Atkins's apartment?"

I expected Richard to jump up and object. The driver had no knowledge he ever went to Jeannie Atkins's apartment. But Richard sat quiet and let the driver answer.

"They went upstairs together at ten o'clock. Richard Rosenberg came out alone at a quarter to twelve."

"How do you place the time?"

"That's my job. Keeping track of the hours. I was contracted for six. By the time Mr. Rosenberg came out, I knew I was going over. I actually got paid for seven."

"Richard Rosenberg was upstairs with the decedent for an hour and forty-five minutes?"

"Yes, he was."

"And didn't come out until a quarter to twelve?"

"That's right."

"What did you do then?"

"I drove him home to his apartment in the Village. Dropped him off at twenty minutes past twelve."

"Did he go inside?"

"He did."

"And how did you know this was his apartment?"

"That's the address where I always picked him up and the address where I always dropped him off. And it's the address on his account."

"Thank you. No further questions."

I couldn't wait for the cross-examination. Thanks to my detective work, Richard was in a good position to show the driver was lying about the time.

He didn't.

Richard didn't challenge him on the time at all. Richard sauntered up to the witness stand and greeted the driver as casually as if he were picking him up for a ride.

"You drove us to diner at Peter Luger's?"

"That's right."

"That's in Brooklyn?"

"Yes, it is."

"And you drove us back to her apartment on Fifth Avenue?"

"That's right."

"That would be a twenty- to thirty-minute ride?"

"Sometime longer. Depending on traffic."

"Did you hear what we were talking about in the back seat?"

"That's not my job."

"I know it isn't. I'm asking if you did."

"No, I did not."

"Is there a glass partition in the car?"

"No, there isn't."

"So you could hear perfectly well. Particularly if we raised our voices. Are you telling me we didn't?"

"I don't remember."

"Why not?"

"I told you. It's not my job. And it wasn't important."

"When you learned she'd been killed, did you try to remember then?"

"I don't recall."

"So nothing stuck out? I didn't say something like, 'I'm going to kill you as soon as we get home'?"

"Objection."

"Overruled."

"No, you did not."

"Good. I didn't recall saying anything of that nature, but you never know. So, did you hear *anything* from the back seat?"

The witness hesitated.

"Ah!" Richard said. "You thought of something. What is it?"

"I seem to recall her giggling."

"Yes, I do too. Do you have any idea why?"

"No, I do not."

"Was it sexual in nature?"

"No."

"Ah, so *that* you know. Is the reason you know it wasn't sexual in nature because you would be sure to know if it was?"

"Objection."

"Sustained."

"So, as far as you were concerned, the ride back was completely harmonious?"

"I would have to say yes."

"You would *have* to? You mean you say so reluctantly? You feel the need to apologize for anything that might undermine the prosecutor's case?"

"Objection."

"Your Honor, the bias of the witness is entirely relevant."

"Overruled."

"I say reluctantly because I don't remember well, and I am reluctant to characterize the trip as anything at all."

Richard nodded approvingly. "Good answer. No further questions."

"Any redirect, Mr. Drexler?"

The ADA, perhaps surprised that Richard had stopped there, had to think for a moment. "Ah, no, Your Honor."

"Very well. Call your next witness."

"Call Ramon Castella."

The doorman took the stand, testified to Richard's picking up Jeannie Atkins around dinnertime and returning with her in the vicinity of nine thirty.

"And did he go upstairs with her?"

"He did."

"Was this a usual occurrence?"

"Yes, it was."

"So you're certain it was Richard Rosenberg?"

"Oh, yes."

"And did you see Mr. Rosenberg leave?"

"I did."

"What time was that?"

"Approximately eleven forty-five."

"How do you fix the time?"

"My shift ends at midnight. I was watching the clock to see how long till I got off."

"You are positive in your identification?"

"Oh, yes. He'd been there many times."

"Your witness."

Richard approached the witness. His manner was casual. "You fix the time by the fact you were about to go off duty?"

"That's right."

"That was uppermost in your mind?"

"Not so much I didn't see you go out."

"I understand. But that was your main concern?"

"It wasn't my *main* concern. It was a reason to be aware of the time."

"I understand. So you saw me go out quite clearly?"

"Yes, I did."

"You're very observant, aren't you?'

"I beg your pardon?"

"Well, that's your job, isn't it? To screen the people coming in, size them up, tell the tenant who's there. And not just their name. If a disreputable person were seeking admittance, you would manage to convey that fact, would you not?"

"That's right."

"So, you are a trained observer. Particularly of the people going in and out?"

"Yes, I am."

"What was my manner?"

"What?"

"Was there anything in my manner that rang alarm bells in your mind? Was I agitated? Flustered? Upset? Did I look like I just stabbed a naked woman with a knife?"

The doorman frowned. "Not that I noticed."

"And you're trained to notice, right? Anything out of the ordinary you notice. You're on it like a cat on a mouse."

The doorman looked uncomfortable.

"Objection, Your Honor. I don't hear a question."

"At the time I left the building were you aware Jeannie Atkins was dead?"

"Of course not."

"That's good, because she wasn't. When did you learn she'd been killed in the night?"

"The next morning. The super went in with a key."

"The next morning. Well, that explains it. Your descriptions of when I left are what you remember looking *back* on the incident. You didn't notice at the time."

"No, I noticed."

"You noticed me leave?"

"Yes."

"And it was an important enough event that you remembered the exact time?"

"I told you why."

"Yes, you were about to go off duty. Tell me, who else came out of the building between the time I came out and the time your shift ended."

The doorman blinked. "Who else?"

"The people who came out after me would be even closer to the time you went off duty. I would think they would be uppermost in your mind. Who were they?"

"Objection, Your Honor."

"Overruled. The witness may answer."

The doorman looked very irritated. "It's a long time ago. I don't remember."

"Ah," Richard said. "You don't remember." He smiled. "I had a feeling you didn't."

#

"Recall Tony Fuller."

The super took the stand again.

"I remind you you're still under oath," Judge Hollins said.

"Mr. Fuller," Richard said, "on the night before you went in and found Jeannie Atkins's body, did you man the front desk?"

"Yes, I did."

"From when till when?"

"From midnight until eight in the morning."

"You relieved the doorman, Ramon Castella, who went off duty at that time?"

"That's right."

"And during the time you were on the desk, did anyone come to see Jeannie Atkins?"

"No, they did not."

"How do you know?"

"Anyone wishing to call on Jeannie Atkins would have to stop at the front desk and ask to see her. And I would call upstairs and ask her if she wanted me to send them up."

"How can you be sure no one did?"

"Our tenants don't have that many visitors after midnight. If someone would have called on her at that hour, I would have known."

"And no one called on Jeannie Atkins between midnight and eight A.M.?"

"That's right."

"No further questions."

Richard paused just long enough for the super to think he was going to get away again. "I have one or two questions, Mr. Fuller."

"Sure."

"You say you're on the desk from midnight till eight A.M.?"

"That's right."

"You're alone on the desk?"

"What do you mean?"

"Well, there's no one else in the lobby. Just you."

"I assure you I'm telling the truth."

"Never said you weren't. I'm just pointing out you were the only one there."

"I don't know *any* building has two people on the midnight shift."

"Or on the day shift either," Richard said.

"Huh?"

"When Mr. Castella is on the desk, there's no one else in the lobby, is there? But he's not alone. Because you're in your apartment in case he needs help."

"Exactly."

"And your apartment is on the ground floor, so you're right there."

"That's right."

"When the doorman's on the desk, is the front door locked?"

"No, it's not."

"How about when you're on the desk, from twelve to eight? Is it locked then?"

"Yes, it is."

"I thought it was," Richard said. "Because Mr. Castella mentioned locking it when he went off duty. So, what happens if someone wants to get in?"

"The tenants have a key."

"I'm talking about visitors."

"They ring the bell. I buzz them in, stop them at the desk, ask them where they're going."

"I see. And that's why you would remember if someone called on Jeannie Atkins?"

"That's right."

"When you buzz them in, do you have to go to the front door?"

"Of course not."

"Where's the buzzer you press?"

"Under the desktop."

"And is the front door glass?"

"Yes, it is."

"So you can see who's out there before you buzz them in."

"That's right."

"Is there any other place to buzz them in from?"

"No, just the front desk."

"And when they ring the doorbell, does that ring at the front desk?"

"Yes, it does."

"Does it ring anywhere else?"

The super hesitated.

"I gather it does. And where would that be?"

"In my apartment."

"The front doorbell rings in your apartment?"

"Yes."

"Why?"

"So I know if someone's at the door."

"But isn't it the person at the desk who needs to know if someone's at the door?"

"It rings there too."

"I understand. But why would it ring in your apartment if someone's always on the front desk?"

"For security purposes."

"Security purposes? I'm not sure I understand this. If someone's on the front desk and you hear the front doorbell, do you leave your apartment and go out and serve as backup?"

"Of course not."

"Then what is the point of the bell?"

"When I'm on the front desk, if I have to run to the bathroom, I don't want to leave someone standing outside the front door."

"So, the buzzer in your apartment is the backup system?"

"That's right."

"So, if I rang the doorbell at four in the morning, you would be at the front desk?"

The super hesitated. "I thought you had a key."

"Really? Why did you think that?"

"You did, didn't you?"

"I'm not on the stand. Why did *you* think I had a key?"

"That's what I heard."

"Ah. Hearsay. Not admissible. But always illuminating. Who did you hear that from?"

"Objection, Your Honor."

"On what grounds?"

"Hearsay."

"What the witness may have been told is hearsay. Who told it to him is not."

"The witness will answer."

"I heard it from the cops."

Richard smiled. "I thought so. That was, of course, *after* the murder."

"That's right."

"How did you know I had a key before Jeannie Atkins was killed?"

"Well, it stood to reason."

"It stood to reason? I do not believe that's considered conclusive evidence."

"Well, if you didn't have a key, the girl was stringing you along."

The spectators laughed. A few jurors smiled.

Richard smiled himself. "Touché. Not a valid legal reason but certainly entertaining." He raised one finger. "For the sake of argument. Say I didn't have a key or at least didn't have it with me—if I buzzed the door at four in the morning, you would be at the front desk?"

"Unless I was in my apartment. In which case, I would hear the buzzer."

"But you couldn't see what was going on in the lobby."

"I always leave my apartment door open."

Richard nodded. "Yes. That's what I thought. No further questions."

Tony Fuller left the stand.

"Call your next witness."

"Call Alexander Redfield."

41

The fingerprint expert was smug and arrogant. You could tell before he opened his mouth. But when he rattled off his qualifications as if he were royalty addressing the unwashed masses, it was particularly galling to realize he was about to nail Richard's ass to the wall.

"Now, Mr. Redfield, did you examine the fingerprints found in the victim's apartment?"

Mr. Redfield smiled a superior smile. "As to where the fingerprints were found, I have no knowledge. I examined fingerprints provided to me that had been marked with that designation."

"I understand. I hand you these photographs that have been marked for identification as People's Exhibits nine through twelve, and ask if they are the fingerprints that you examined."

Redfield looked them over carefully before nodding. "They are."

"And how were the fingerprints you worked on labeled?"

"They were labeled as coming from the apartment of the decedent, Jeannie Atkins."

"And where in particular were these fingerprints labeled as coming from?"

"From the decedent's knife."

"The knife that has been marked for identification as People's Exhibit Two?"

"That is correct."

"How many fingerprints did you find?"

"There were five legible prints on the knife. I should say four and a half. The print of the little finger was clear enough to discern it as coming from the same set. But only half of it was actually visible."

"And did you attempt to match those fingerprints with the fingerprints of any particular person?"

"I did."

"Were you able to do so?"

"The prints are unquestionably a match for the prints on the fingers of the right hand of the defendant, Richard Rosenberg."

"Each and every print?"

"Each and every print."

"Each and every finger?"

"That is correct."

"Did the prints prove beyond a shadow of a doubt that the defendant, Richard Rosenberg, held this knife?"

"Absolutely. The position of the prints is consistent with him gripping it with his right hand."

"Thank you. No further questions."

Judge Hollins turned to the defense table. Almost ironically he said, "Mr. Rosenberg?"

Richard approached the witness, stopped, frowned. "Doctor, I'm a little bit confused about this."

Redfield bristled. "I am not a doctor."

Richard raised his eyebrows in surprise. "You're not a doctor? I thought you were a doctor."

"No, I'm an expert technician."

"Oh. An expert *technician*."

"I have a degree in criminology."

"Ah, that would explain why you think you know about my fingerprints."

"I *do* know about your fingerprints. All five fingers of your right hand were on that knife. You did not question me on my qualifications, but I would be delighted to demonstrate for the jury the points of similarity that prove, conclusively, that those are your prints."

"I'm sure you would. That's your field of expertise. That's what you do. You are unquestionably an expert at matching one fingerprint with another. There are different standards of comparison, but I believe eighteen points of similarity are beyond any requirement to prove an identical match. I am sure you found many *more* than the minimum and could spend a great deal of time pointing them out. That would certainly be sufficient to justify your conclusion that those are my prints."

"That's not a conclusion. That's a fact."

"That's not a conclusion?"

"No."

"That's funny. I thought *all* fingerprint matches were conclusions. Or do you start with a predetermined outcome?"

"Very clever, Mr. Rosenberg, but you know what I mean, and I'm sure the jurors do too."

Redfield smiled at the jury. One or two of the jurors smiled back.

Richard smiled too. "So. We are all in agreement. Those five fingerprints on the knife are mine."

Redfield blinked. After the tenor of the cross-examination, he hardly had expected Richard to concede the point.

"So," Richard said. "My prints are on the knife. I take no issue with that part of your testimony. I do take issue with your conclusion that they prove I held the knife."

"You may take issue if you want, but the facts are the facts."

"You claim the facts show I held the knife?"

"Absolutely. The facts bear that out. Your fingerprints are not scattered willy-nilly all over the knife. All are on the handle. None are on the blade. And the prints are arranged, in order. The index finger, middle finger, ring finger, and pinky are together, in order, with the opposable thumb neatly opposing them on the other side."

"Well," Richard said, "since you were eager to demonstrate for the jury, perhaps you could demonstrate that."

"I beg your pardon?"

Richard picked up the knife from the evidence table. "I hand you a knife that has been marked for identification People's Exhibit Two." He reached in his pocket. "And I hand you a roll of masking tape and a pen. I am going to ask you if you would mark on the knife exactly where the prints that you are testifying to were found."

"May I refer to the photos?"

"Of course."

The witness began tearing off strips of masking tape.

"And would you please indicate which is which. *I* for index, *M* for middle, *R* for ring, *P* for pinky, *T* for thumb."

Redfield marked the knife. When he was finished he said, "There."

"And in your opinion those are the prints of a person holding the knife?"

"The prints speak for themselves."

"I'm sure they do, Mr. Redfield, but their voice is not in the record. Would you be so good as to pick up the knife, hold it in your right hand, and demonstrate that you can indeed hold the knife with your fingers in that position?"

Redfield placed his fingers on the knife, gripped it tightly in his right hand.

"Thank you," Richard said. "I think I would have to concede that you are indeed able to hold the knife."

"Of course I am."

"Since we can't see you holding it in the record, I ask if this is what we see: you holding the knife tightly in your right hand. Your fingers, as you say, are on the knife in order. Your index finger is closest to the blade, with your middle finger behind it, then your ring finger and your pinky. Is that right?"

"Yes, it is."

"And your thumb encircles the handle, holding the knife tight."

"Yes, it does."

"That's fine, Mr. Redfield. Would you mind doing one more thing? ADA Drexler is sitting down at his table. Would you please walk up behind him and stab him in the back?"

There was a stunned silence.

ADA Drexler lunged from his seat. "Objection, Your Honor!"

"You object to being stabbed in the back?" Richard said.

Judge Hollins banged the gavel. "Your objection is not necessary, Mr. Drexler. No one is stabbing anyone in the back in my courtroom."

"May I be heard, Your Honor?" Richard said.

"You may not. What you are suggesting is a ridiculous stunt. You know I won't allow it. The question borders on contempt of court."

"The question is withdrawn, Your Honor." Richard turned back to the witness. "Now then, Mr. Redfield, you are still holding the knife in the position in which you claim I held it, with all of your fingers lined up according to my prints."

"That's right."

"So let me ask you something. Is that the way you would hold a knife to stab it into someone's heart? I don't mean you personally, you wouldn't do such a thing, but if you were going to, would you hold that knife in that fashion?"

"Absolutely. I have a firm grip and would have no problem stabbing the victim."

"Well, you could probably stab her in the stomach," Richard said. "But how would you stab her in the heart? If she were standing up, it's practically impossible. Even if she was sitting down, the angle's all wrong. You would have to twist yourself into a pretzel or break your arm at the wrist in order to stab the knife down. The only way you could stab it down is if your fingers were reversed on the knife, with your pinky finger closest to the blade, then your ring, middle, and index. Holding the knife in that fashion, you could stab the knife down just fine, whether the victim was standing, sitting, or lying down. Isn't that right, Mr. Redfield?"

"Objection, Your Honor. Counsel is making an argument in the guise of a question."

"It's a yes or no question, Your Honor."

Judge Hollins took a breath. "The question is adroitly framed but certainly legal. The witness may answer."

"The fingerprints indicate you held the knife. The manner in which the wound was inflicted is not my field of expertise."

"Clearly," Richard said.

I was relieved to see a couple of the jurors snickered.

"I would still like an answer. You have testified that I held the knife. That testimony goes beyond fingerprint identification. That is a conclusion on your part as to what the fingerprints indicate. Which, if I understand you correctly, is not your field of expertise. But since you offered that opinion, I should think you should be able to defend it by explaining to the jury why that opinion is justified."

"Objection, Your Honor. That's not a question."

"Let me ask a question. Mr. Redfield, you testified, did you not, that I held the knife, moreover that I could 'absolutely' have stabbed the victim holding it in that manner. Do you recall that?"

"You're paraphrasing my statement."

"Well, let's have the court reporter read it back."

The court reporter flipped back in her notes.

"Mr. Rosenberg: 'So let me ask you something. Is that the way you would hold a knife to stab it into someone's heart? I don't mean you personally, you wouldn't do such a thing, but if you were going to, would you hold that knife in that fashion?'

Mr. Redfield: 'Absolutely. I have a firm grip and would have no problem stabbing the victim.'"

The witness was beginning to sweat. He ran his finger inside his shirt collar.

"That's what I thought you said. Absolutely. Though, by your own testimony, you are only a fingerprint expert and not a medical examiner who examined the fatal wound, you expressed the unequivocal opinion that a person could stab the victim holding the knife in the manner in which you are holding it. You have stated that absolutely, beyond a shadow of a doubt, I could have held the knife in that fashion and delivered the fatal blow." Richard paused, let that sink in. "Would you like to reconsider your answer?"

"No. My answer is correct, no matter how much you want to twist my words. And I think the jury understands that."

This time there were no answering smiles.

"I think they do too," Richard said. "No further questions."

42

Richard looked utterly drained. He leaned back in his desk chair, loosened his tie. He absently swiveled the chair back and forth with his feet.

"That went well," I said.

He stopped swiveling, fixed me with a cold eye. "Well? You call that well? They've got me holding the knife."

"Yeah. In a position where you couldn't have used it."

"You know it, I know it, the expert witness knows it. You think the jury knows it?"

"They were responding to you."

"To me? They weren't responding to me. They were responding to *him*."

"What?"

"The fingerprint expert. He's a total asshole. I took him down a notch and the jury liked to see it. That doesn't mean they're buyin' the bullshit."

"But it's not bullshit."

"Sure it is."

"You couldn't have held the knife like that."

"I clearly did."

"To eat dinner. Not to kill someone."

"That's a technicality. It sounds good, until we move on to something else. When we start summing up, what will the jury remember? My prints were on the knife."

"This isn't going to verdict."

"Oh?" Richard cocked his head. "What, you're going to find the real killer?"

"I didn't say that."

"Then I can't see them dropping the case."

"I could see the judge issuing a directed verdict."

"Not in my favor. Wake up, Stanley. The judge may give me a few props for cross-examination. That doesn't mean he's on my side. Far from it. Hollins is a hanging judge. Likes his defendants boiled alive. He's the little kid looking in the lobster cage. In the seafood restaurant, with the lobsters swimming around. I don't like that. Not my style. I don't want to develop a personal relationship with my dinner. I just want it to arrive on the plate. The kid's different. He'd name the sucker, give it to the chef. That's Judge Hollins. And I'm a very juicy lobster."

"But—"

Richard waved his hand. "Hey, hey. Let's not fight over how well it's going. It ain't over till it's over. And it ain't over."

"So, what's next?"

"I'm going to see what they throw at me next, and you're going to look in on Global Bank, see if there's any progress on that front."

"You think it's important?"

"I don't know what's important."

43

My confidante had worked her magic. Juror four was talking to me again. Not that he wasn't hesitant. Not that he wasn't constantly looking around to make sure some beefy cop wasn't about to lift him up by the sharp lapels of his shiny coat, but at least he was talkative.

"Where you been?" he said, as I walked up to him.

I wasn't surprised. My confidante had gloated at his conversion and latched onto me to take the credit as I was barely in the door. She wanted to know what else she could do, and I was at a total loss. As far as I was concerned the one trial had nothing to do with the other, and even if they did, numbered jurors couldn't have mattered less. Still, I went through the motions. If I hadn't, my confidante never would have forgiven me.

I told myself it was for Richard, and tried to make me believe it. "I got a better trial," I said.

"Right," he said. "Murder trial."

"Yeah."

"Gotta be better than this. Probably take longer, though."

I didn't point out that a trial longer than this one would probably make the *Guinness Book of World Records*. "Yeah," I said. "It probably just seems shorter on account of the sex and violence."

"Yeah. I saw it in the *Post*. There was semen on the body. Was that your friend's?"

"I'm not really comfortable discussing a friend's semen."

"Wuss," he said. "So, the guy really fucked her. Or, actually, according to the *Post*—"

"You can't believe what you read in the *Post*," I told him.

"That don't make it wrong. I mean, there really was a headless man in a topless bar, wasn't there?"

"There's plenty of mindless ones. So how's your sex life here? Any luck with juror twelve?"

He made a face. "Cold fish. Lotta potential, no play. It's like as soon as I got put on the jury she didn't want to have anything to do with me."

I frowned. "Put on the jury?"

"I was an alternate. Till juror four dropped out. Not his fault. That guy really did have a medical condition. Not like juror seven, who tried to fake it. But Sammy caught mono and everyone freaked out. Judge couldn't boot him off the jury fast enough. Thought he'd infect us all and that would be that. And we were already five weeks into the trial. You can bet nobody wanted to go through that again."

"I don't understand," I said.

"What?"

"You said juror twelve wouldn't speak to you because you got put on the jury. I would think that would be a reason why she *would* speak to you. You were on the bench, and now you're a member of the team."

"Well, you're not on the bench. You're sitting in the jury box. You're just in the seats that don't matter. The way I understand it, you get through the whole trial without being bumped up, they let you go before deliberation. I was hoping that would happen. But, oh, no, Sammy's gotta get mono and no one wants to take a chance with that. Too contagious. Mono a mono, you know what I mean?"

"Not at all."

"You know, like a one-on-one fight."

"I get the play on words, I just miss the relevance."

"Huh?"

"Never mind. What I don't understand is why would that make her *less* interested in you? It's like you were just an alternate and now you joined the team."

"Yeah, but I hadn't joined her team. I'd *left* her team."

"Huh?"

"Don't you get it?" He looked at me as if he couldn't believe I was so incredibly thick. "*She* was an alternate."

44

I hunted up my confidante. She was bubbling over. I was afraid she'd jump me right there in the courtroom.

"Cooperated, didn't he?" she said. "Did I do it or what?"

"Yeah, he cooperated. Now I got another lead I need help with."

"I'm your girl. Whaddya need?"

"Ron was an alternate. Then he got bumped up to the jury."

"Right."

"Juror twelve was an alternate. She got bumped up to the jury sometime after Ron did."

She frowned. "So?"

"What happened to the juror she replaced?"

"The juror she replaced?"

"Yeah."

She shrugged. "I don't know. She just replaced him."

"Why?"

"What do you mean, why?"

"Ron replaced juror four because he had mono. What about juror twelve? Did he have mono?"

"Good lord, no. Two jurors, it's an epidemic. Would have closed us down."

"So what happened?"

"I don't remember."

"But you can find out. I need the juror's name and address. And I need to know why he got bounced. Can you do that for me?"

She looked offended. "Yeah, I can do it. It's just routine."

"Yeah, but I can't do it. Will you?"

"Sure." She didn't look happy. "Don't you have anything else? Something important?"

"This may be routine, but it's important."

"Why?"

I shook my head. "I don't know."

"You holdin' out on me?"

"On my confidante? Never."

"So what's the deal with juror twelve?"

I sighed. "I have no idea."

45

I didn't want to give her my phone number. We have an unlisted number because Alice doesn't want the crazies I deal with in the course of my work calling me at home. In this I heartily concur. The only inconvenience of the unlisted number is sometimes people we want to have find us can't.

My confidante did not fall into that category. I tend to attract stalkers, needy codependent types who call me at the least provocation in an attempt to worm their way into my life. The law clerk fit the description in spades. That, coupled with her fascination with me as a private eye, would have been more than enough to disqualify her. Her none-too-subtle sexual overtures sealed the deal. There were few people I would have less rather called me at home. At that moment I couldn't think of any, but there must have been some.

At any rate, my confidante couldn't look up the information until after court and I couldn't wait, as I was due at Richard's office for our daily postmortem. Since I was missing his afternoon courtroom session, I was eager to hear. So I reluctantly left her to her task, saying I'd see her in the morning. If that crushed her, I wouldn't have known it. She must have had another man on the side. I wondered if he was a PI.

Richard wasn't bothered by the delay. He seemed pleased with my progress but didn't hold out a lot of hope for its amounting to anything. I might have been insulted, but I didn't hold out much hope either.

As for the trial, ADA Drexler hadn't produced a smoking gun, but nothing had swung in Richard's direction. Kind of a glass half full situation.

I took the whole mess home to Alice, hoping she'd be able to put her inimitable spin on the situation. I think she did. I say *think*, because she was distracting me in another one of my loose-fitting pocket t-shirts, which was about all I could hope for; as I had not been getting much lately. Unless, of course, the law clerk came through.

"The Alternate Juror," Alice said. "No wonder you're so hot on the idea. It practically *sounds* like a noir murder mystery."

"Or a Perry Mason title."

"Except for no alliteration."

"Lots of the titles weren't. *Curious Bride. Fugitive Nurse. Bigamous Spouse. Runaway Corpse. Howling Dog. Lame Canary.*"

Alice pulled her shirt up to her neck.

My mouth fell open, and I started for her.

She pulled her shirt down, put up her hand. "Don't get excited. It was the only way to stop you."

"Alice."

"You have a lead. It's the type that would appeal to a reader of mystery fiction. The problem is, in real life so many of these leads, aren't."

"You don't think it is?"

"No, I'm just telling you not to get your hopes up. You get a lot of leads. Most of them go nowhere. And just because a lead that appears to go nowhere is suddenly saved by a dramatic plot twist, it doesn't make it any more likely."

"I understand. It doesn't necessarily mean anything. I know that."

"I know you know that," Alice said. "It doesn't mean you believe it."

"Right. Alice, did you find anything encouraging in what I said?"

"Is Richard in jail yet?"

"No."

"There you are."

I was somewhat torn. Much as I wanted to check on the status of juror twelve, I had missed a day in court and wanted to hear Richard.

I was somewhat disappointed. After the fireworks with the fingerprint expert, the testimony seemed tame.

It was largely just piling on. Detectives testified to processing the crime scene. The resultant fingerprints were categorized and proved to be—surprise, surprise—Richard Rosenberg's. Why they bothered when they had his prints on the knife was beyond me.

I asked Richard during a ten-minute recess.

He seemed surprised by the question. "It connects me to the crime."

"How does it connect you to the crime?"

"It proves I was in the apartment."

"The murder weapon proves you were in the apartment."

"The murder weapon proves I touched the knife. The knife could have been planted in the apartment."

"Are you serious?"

"Hey, it's something I could argue. Not that I'm going to. If there was one person on the jury who would believe *that*, I'd be amazed. Hell, if there was one person *in America* who'd believe that, I'd be amazed."

"Even so. They've got the doorman, the super, the driver. There's no lack of evidence that you were in that apartment."

"Those people never actually saw me go in."

"Is that what you're going to argue?"

"Are you kidding me? The jurors would think I'm a moron."

"You're willing to concede you were in the apartment?"

"Of course."

"So what's the point?"

"It's evidence against me, that's all. The jury wants to find me guilty. The prosecutor's trying to make it easy on them. Evidence I was in the apartment adds nothing to the case, except in the jurors' minds it's more evidence against me. The fact it doesn't prove anything else is lost on them. All they know is, for another day the prosecutor brought out facts against me."

"That can't be the way it works."

"Why? Because it isn't fair? Because it isn't logical? Because it doesn't conform to your sense of what's right? Politicians go on television every day and answer direct questions with flagrant lies. They know they're lies. The interviewers know they're lies. The people watching know they're lies. But does that matter? Not at all. A million people hear that statement. Some of them think it's true. Some of them don't care. Some of them believe anything they see on TV. Jurors tend to believe anything they hear in court. Unless it's the defendant saying it, of course. They know *he's* a lying sack of shit."

Richard shrugged. "This is even better. It's not a lie. It's the absolute truth. The prosecutor is putting on uncontested evidence linking me to the victim. The jurors don't say so what? The jurors shake their heads and say how *could* he?"

"So how do you win?"

"My PI saves me at the last moment."

"No, really."

"Stanley, I haven't even begun to put on my case yet."

"What's your case?"

"Well, that's the thing."

"What?"

"I have no idea."

47

The Global Bank trial recessed at noon.

My confidante was the first one out the door. She grabbed me, whisked me off into the shadows. A rather ostentatious move for a clandestine informant. If anyone noticed, I didn't know how I could cover that without feigning a romantic attachment.

I wondered if that was her idea.

"Did you get it?" I said.

"Of course I got it."

"So what's the story?"

"The juror's Ralph Hogan. He got excused from the jury five days after Ron got put on."

"Five days?"

"Five court days. That's one calendar week."

"What'd he get excused for?"

"I'm not sure. But it wasn't mono. He had a letter from his doctor. But I can't access medical records."

"You weren't there when it happened?"

"No, it was done in chambers. The law clerks weren't privy to the conversation. Only the attorneys."

"You got an address?"

"Of course I do."

She pulled a folded paper out of her cleavage. That was I surprise. I hadn't noticed she had cleavage. She hadn't, really, just a *V* in her blouse. She'd managed to unbutton one more button when no one was looking. I certainly wasn't. At least until she pulled the paper out of her bra.

Her eyes were gleaming. She glanced around to see if anyone was looking, then sidled up closer to me.

"Here you go."

She was shielding the paper by holding it close to her chest. It was almost impossible to take it without accidentally copping a feel.

I unfolded the paper. For my confidante's benefit, I gave it a brief, surreptitious look. On it was a 212 number and an address on East Ninety-eighth Street.

"How about a business address?"

"He's self-employed."

"What's he do?"

"Freelance photographer."

"Works from home?"

"I would imagine. Anyway, there's no business address."

It wasn't easy escaping her clutches. I had to feign a trip to the men's room. It wasn't that hard, since I actually had to go. I was just afraid she'd be waiting when I came out.

She wasn't, and I headed for the elevator bank. The ADA and the attractive attorney weren't lunching together. She was accompanied by her co-counsel and her client. I wound up in the same car, wondered if I'd learn anything useful. I didn't hold out much hope. Elevator conversations were notoriously dull. This one was no different. The defendant didn't say, "Wow, you really got them fooled," and the attorney didn't say, "Don't mention that second offshore account." Just some generic speculation about whether it was raining. Apparently the gentleman didn't like raindrops on his five-thousand-dollar suit.

It wasn't raining. We reached the street, headed in our separate directions. No portentous words had been uttered, no secrets were revealed. All the elevator ride showed me was that I was on a fool's errand, that nothing about the Global Banking case had anything to do with Richard's, that I was wasting my time.

I didn't need an elevator ride to tell me that.

48

Ralph Hogan lived in a fourth-floor walk-up on East Ninety-eighth, the type of apartment that was rarer and rarer these days, an unprepossessing railroad flat with all the space of a midsize studio apartment with none of the amenities. For me, the lack of elevator was the worst. I didn't like walk-ups when I was young, and I positively hated them now. If I'd lived in the damn place, I'd have never gone out.

Security wasn't so hot either. The street door was open. That was a blessing. I didn't really want to explain my business over an intercom. On the other hand, that meant I had to trudge up three flights of stairs just to see if he was home.

I was puffing by the time I reached his door. Not the type of thing I'd like to admit to Alice. She'd put me on some regimen of training. I don't train well. I don't even jog. For me to run, a ball has to be involved.

I found the apartment, which wasn't hard. There was only one per floor. Not that they were large. It was just a skinny building.

There was no bell, so I knocked on the door.

It swung open.

Uh oh.

I read mystery novels, and if a door swings opens it's because the occupant is dead. I wanted to talk to juror twelve, not find his body. Ridiculous as the possibility might be. Juror twelve was the longest of long shots.

I knocked again. Pushed the door open. Called his name.

There was no answer.

I had absolutely no reason to search his apartment. For one thing, I wouldn't know what I was looking for. And with my luck, he'd come home and catch me doing it. Or some neighbor would see me go in and call the cops. Of course there wasn't a neighbor on the floor, but with my luck . . .

I pushed the door open and found myself in the kitchen.

The kitchen?

The percentage of apartments with front doors that open into the kitchen is not high. This kitchen also had a bathtub in it. How much would that drop the rent? Or was it retro enough to be a selling point?

To the left were wide-open doorways to two more rooms.

I wasn't about to hang out in the apartment. Just a quick perusal to see if any clue jumped out at me.

The bed had not been made. I was not tempted to make it. I was not tempted to lie down in it either. It ponged a bit. The windows were not open, and the whole room smelled musty.

I walked around the end of the bed and stopped short.

A young man lay on the floor.

From his cold, glassy-eyed stare I could tell my interview with Ralph Hogan was not going to go well.

49

Sergeant Thurman was eloquent. That bears repeating. It was practically a first in the annals of crime detection. But for the usually monosyllabic officer, his performance was off the chart.

He began with sarcastic applause, in itself wittier than his usual remark, and launched right in to, "And the award for best performance by a private investigator at a crime scene at which he had no business appearing goes to this douche bag here."

Good lord, had Thurman just made that up? Or had he seen it in a movie somewhere? I figured the latter. There were so many these days, practically everything had been said in a movie somewhere.

"So, got your story ready?"

"No story. I just walked in and found him dead."

"Oh, you had an appointment with him?"

"No."

"Called and told him you were coming?"

"No."

"Buzzed him on the intercom?"

"No."

"Rang his doorbell?"

"I knocked on the door and called hello."

"And he said come in, so you walked in and found him dead?"

"The door was open. I stuck my head in, looked around."

"Why?"

"To see if anything was wrong."

"Why'd you think something was wrong?"

"It's not normal to leave your door open."

"People leave their door open. It doesn't mean they're dead."

"This one did."

"What's this guy's connection with Rosenberg?"

"There's no connection with Rosenberg."

"Then why are you here?"

"He was a juror on the Global Bank case."

Thurman slammed me up against the wall. No mean feat in the small, cramped kitchen, but Thurman managed. Pans rattled.

"You son of a bitch! You tell me to my face this has nothing to do with Rosenberg."

"It doesn't."

"Why were you investigating Global Banking?"

"Because of Jeannie Atkinson."

Thurman slammed me up against the wall again. This time it had lost some of its appeal.

"That's the Rosenberg case! You want to live long enough to hear the verdict, you give me a straight answer!"

"I stumbled on something else. It's not what I was working on, but I'm running it down."

"What?"

"The Global Banking case. Jurors are dropping like flies. Last time I was there, the judge refused to let a juror off, even with a doctor's note. Said he wanted the doctor in court to testify."

"So what?"

"You're a cop, right?"

Thurman rolled his eyes. "Oh, fucking genius."

"You find something odd, you wanna know."

"That's my job."

"Mine too."

"Bullshit. You got one job. Anything else is none of your business."

"Fine. It's none of my business. Jurors on this case were dropping out. I thought it was odd. Maybe it's got nothing to do with Rosenberg. On the other hand, it can't hurt. And, frankly, I don't know anything that helps. So I followed the lead. I'm as surprised as you are it panned out."

"Panned out? Is that what you call it? Panned out? You stick your nose in and the guy is dead."

"I don't think it's my fault."

"Of course, you don't. You'd much rather we charged someone else."

"You suspect me of this crime?"

"You got a better idea?"

"Yeah."

"What's that?"

"Don't suspect me of this crime."

That earned me another trip into the wall.

"Wrong answer. You got one more chance to come up with the right answer, or you're going downtown."

"The right answer is I haven't a clue. You wanna charge me, charge me. I can't tell you something I don't know."

"Tell me how you got here."

I was gonna say subway, but my shoulder was getting awful sore. "I was talking to some of the jurors."

"I told you not to do that."

"You wanna hear how I got here?"

"What about the jurors?"

"A couple of the ones I was talking to were alternates. Made me wonder about the guys they replaced."

"What about 'em?"

"One guy had mono. Can't argue with that. The other guy, no one was quite sure." I jerked my thumb. "That's him in there."

Thurman blinked. "That's all you had to go on?"

"That's all I had to go on."

"That's nothing."

"Right. The guy must still be alive."

Thurman waffled. On the one hand, it was fun throwing me up against the wall. On the other, he did have a crime to solve.

"When'd you get this lead?"

"Yesterday."

"Why'd you wait?"

"It wasn't urgent. As you pointed out, I have another case."

"You *had* another case. Your boss is screwed. He was with her when she died, and his prints are on the knife."

"You think that's conclusive?"

"Damn right it is."

"Then why doesn't Drexler rest?"

"I'm not an ADA."

"No shit."

Once more unto the wall, dear friends. You'd think I'd learn.

"So," Thurman said, "why'd your boss have to kill him?"

"Huh?"

"Well, I'm assuming it was him. Unless he hired you to do his dirty work."

"You think the crimes are related?"

"I'm sure you do."

"This guy wasn't stabbed, was he?"

"As if you didn't know."

"Just like it."

"Huh?"

"I didn't see any sign of a wound, but I didn't touch the body to look for one. I saw he was dead and got the hell out of there."

"Without touching anything?"

"I'm sure I touched something. If your boys can't find my fingerprints, it means they're not trying. I was in the apartment. I found the body. My fingerprints don't prove anything. They confirm what I already said. Stop changing the subject."

That caught him up short. "*I'm* changing the subject?"

"I asked you what killed him. The way you're evading the question, I figure you don't know."

Thurman glowered ominously. "Maybe someone tried to push him through a wall."

50

I was lucky Richard Rosenberg was out on bail, unlucky he was on trial. He was free to bail me out but only between court appearances.

Actually, bail was not required. Richard said something to someone they didn't like the sound of, and the next thing you know I was free.

"So, who'd you kill?" Richard said as we came down the front steps.

"You don't want to know."

"Regale me. It will be a break from my own troubles."

There was a car from a car service waiting out front. We climbed in the back and I gave him the whole schmear. He listened with an absolutely deadpan face, betraying nothing. Which was disconcerting. I couldn't tell if he was going to thank me, fire me, or burst out crying.

He chose relentless sarcasm. "You launched an investigation into a juror who was no longer on the case and hadn't been for months?"

"That's right."

"On the theory that his departure from the jury might mean something?"

"Yes."

"You based the theory on the fact that jurors tend to drop off this jury more frequently than other juries?"

"What's wrong with that?"

"You heard the case. If you were on that jury, wouldn't you be fighting to get off?"

"I wouldn't be on that jury."

"You would if they took you."

"No one would take me."

"Someone will always take you when you least expect it. That's not the point. With twelve people on the jury not all of them will be happy to be there. Throw a case like this at 'em they'll be committing hari-kari to get off."

"You're right, Richard. It was a stupid idea. Of course it came to nothing."

"Sarcasm? Now you're giving me sarcasm? Yes, the guy died. It doesn't mean he was important. It means you made the killer *think* he was important."

"You think Jeannie Atkins's killer did it?"

"I think *Ralph Hogan's* killer did it. Whether he killed Jeannie Atkins is another matter. For whatever the cause, it's fairly safe to assume you set the wheels in motion. Not much of a reputation for a private investigator. 'The people I talk to die.'"

My beeper went off. It sounded awfully loud in the car, I suppose because Richard was in it. My beeper goes off all the time when I'm driving, and I never give it a thought.

"I can't believe you still wear a beeper," Richard said.

"I don't want to answer the phone when I'm driving."

"You're not driving. Call the office."

I took out my cell phone. "If they try to give me a case, I'm going to lose it."

"You couldn't squeeze in one quick sign-up?" Richard said.

I gave him a look.

"I'm kidding. Call the office."

It wasn't an assignment. It was a message to call MacAullif.

51

"This is bad," MacAullif said.

"I know it's bad."

"I'm not sure you do. What'd you tell Thurman?"

"What do you mean?"

"How'd you account for being interested in the guy?"

"I told him the case had an abnormal number of juror dropouts so I was investigating the jurors that got bounced."

"He buy that?"

"Wouldn't you?"

"I know better. Would I buy it if I didn't know better? Not if you were selling it. I'd figure you had some ulterior motive. I'd figure it was a line you were feeding me so you wouldn't have to tell me what you were really doing. And I'll bet you that's how Thurman figures it."

"No takers."

"If you were spewing bullshit, why'd they let you go?"

"I got a good lawyer."

"What'd you tell him?"

"The truth."

"He buy it?"

"It's the truth."

"What's your point? *I* know it's the truth, and *I* don't buy it. The whole thing makes no sense."

"No shit. They find the murder weapon?"

"What murder weapon? He was probably hit with a blunt object, but that's not official."

"You got a time of death?"

"Haven't heard anything. Doesn't mean they don't know. Couldn't you tell from the corpse?"

"Looked like he'd been dead a while."

MacAullif nodded. "So, he probably died when you opened the door."

"I wish he had."

"Why?"

"Richard was in court."

"So that's how you're thinking."

"I'm not thinking that way. Wanna bet Thurman is?"

"Could Richard have done it?"

"No, Richard couldn't have done it."

"Why not?"

"Because it's so bloody fucking stupid I can't believe we're even talking about it."

"I'm talking in terms of the time element. Was he killed when Richard has an alibi?"

"I know what you were getting at. The answer is probably not. Bad as I am at this shit, it's a good bet he was killed before court resumed this morning."

"I'm sure Richard appreciates your opinion."

"He didn't ask it."

"Why not?"

"He *knows* he didn't do it."

"And he doesn't care what other people think?"

"He can't *do* anything about what other people think."

"That's just stupid."

"Why, because it's true?"

"Don't be an asshole."

"Sorry. I spent the afternoon in jail. It makes me cranky. Why'd you call me down here?"

"To find out how come you tripped over a corpse."

"I'm sorry you don't like the answer."

"It's a nonanswer. You wanna tell me the straight shit?"

I gave MacAullif an expurgated version of the mystery of the number twelve. He didn't take it well. I was afraid he might break Thurman's record for pushing me through the wall.

"Are you out of your fucking mind?" MacAullif said.

"I think the jury's in on that one. It was a stupid idea. I can't believe it's true."

"Who says it's true? You decided A implies B. B happened. Now you decide B implies A."

"Are you sure you're a cop?"

"Forget your fucking numbers game. You decide you want to know why the guy left the jury. When you try to find out, he's dead. So who'd you tell?"

"I didn't tell anyone."

"How'd you find the guy?

"I had one of the law clerks look up the address."

MacAullif groaned. "One of Judge Peters's law clerks? A law clerk who worked with Jeannie Atkins? It doesn't occur to you maybe he's a jealous lover who killed Jeannie Atkins for messing around with Richard Rosenberg? And maybe this juror knew of this connection and the thought of you questioning him throws the guy into a panic?"

"The law clerk is not some young stud lover. It's a dweeby girl thrilled to be playing detective."

"When'd she look up the address?"

"Last night after court."

"Why didn't you go over then?"

"I had a meeting with Richard."

"Why didn't you go when it was over?"

"I didn't have the address. She gave it to me this morning in court."

"But she looked it up last night?"

"Yeah."

MacAullif looked at me pityingly. "Who'd she tell?"

52

Alice agreed with MacAullif. Which is the wrong way to put it. It wasn't so much that she agreed with MacAullif as she disagreed with me.

"You think the numbers are meaningless?"

"I didn't say that," Alice said, a bold statement on her part, since she *had* said that. But I knew better than to contradict her. I could produce a recording of what she actually said, and she'd be able to prove different.

"Well, what *did* you say?"

"I just said they're not important. What's important is the juror's dead. The chance he was killed to keep you from questioning him is far more likely than the chance he was killed because Jeannie Atkins had the number twelve taped to the bottom of her panties drawer.

"Granted, the two things are not mutually exclusive. But the one that's not lifted out of a Nancy Drew book is the one to concentrate on."

"A Nancy Drew book?"

"The Secret of Number Twelve. So, is MacAullif going to shake down the law clerk."

"Not his case."

"Is Thurman?"

"Thurman doesn't know about the law clerk."

"You held out on Thurman?"

"Wouldn't you?"

"No. I wouldn't do anything to put myself in this position."

"You'd let Richard rot?"

"That's unfair."

"Why is it unfair?"

"To make that the choice. Either you do something stupid or you don't wanna help Richard."

"That's not what I said."

"Oh? Please point out where I'm wrong."

I wasn't playing that game. I kept quiet.

"So, you gonna follow up on MacAullif's idea?"

"MacAullif's idea?"

"Finding out who knew you were going to see the juror. After you got through with the number twelve, of course."

"Alice."

"Is the law clerk dependable?"

"Yes."

"She have big tits?"

"She's not attractive."

"Is she an unattractive girl with big tits?"

"I don't think so. I really hadn't noticed."

"She's that unattractive?"

"She's rather plain."

Alice shook her head. "Men."

"What do you mean?"

"She's not sexy so she must be telling the truth?"

I was stunned into silence. If she were attractive, Alice would have said she's got nice tits so she must be telling the truth.

"If she blabbed about it, would she tell you?"

"Of course."

"Really? She wouldn't try to hide the fact that she was unreliable?"

"I think if she realized it was important to me, she'd tell the truth."

"She must be really smitten."

"Alice."

"So why is Thurman handling the case?"

"I'm just really lucky."

"Seriously. Does he think the two cases are related?"

"I don't think he had any idea till he got there."

"I don't know. These stupid types are awfully smart."

If I said that, Alice would have ridiculed me from here to Sunday and regaled her friends with it at every given opportunity. Because she said it, it was perfectly logical, cast in iron, and only an addlebrained fool would think any different.

"Were you questioned by an ADA?"

"I was."

"Did you tell *him* about the number twelve? Did you tell him about the law clerk?"

"No."

"Was it the ADA handling Richard's case?"

"Of course not."

"Why of course not?"

"He was in court prosecuting Richard."

"Was it one of his associates?"

"They all work for the DA."

"Thank you for that illuminating clarification. Was he one of his trial associates on the case?"

"No."

"You don't always recognize people."

"He wasn't from the case."

"What did he want to know?"

"How I happened to find the body."

"What'd you tell him?"

"Same thing I told Thurman."

"Did he buy it?"

"They held me until Richard showed up."

"How about Richard?'

"What do you mean?"

"Did he know this juror?"

My mouth fell open. "Alice."

"Well, he was dating a law clerk."

"Yes, and I'm sure she introduced him to all the jurors on the trail she was working."

"Not all of them. Just this one."

"And why would she introduce him to this one?"

"Same reason he's dead."

That caught me up short. Alice's logic, contrary though it might be to conventional wisdom, natural laws, and anything I might think, has an unfairly high incidence of being sound. What if Richard, the law clerk, and the juror got involved in something, as a result of which two of them died?

"Was it possible? Did Richard know you were questioning this juror?"

My mouth felt dry. I had called him to say I was getting the address of the juror and I might miss court to go see him in the morning. So Richard knew the night before. And he was the only one I'd told.

I pushed the thought out of my head, angrily.

It couldn't be Richard.

The law clerk must have blabbed.

53

My confidante was bouncing off the walls. I was afraid she was going to attack me in open court. Luckily, she waited for recess. She pulled me out in the hallway and demanded, "What did you do? You killed a man, and I helped you do it! I'm an accessory!"

"I didn't kill anyone."

"Oh, no? I give you the guy's name, he winds up dead. And the police catch you in his apartment."

"The police didn't catch me in his apartment."

She rolled her eyes. "Oh. *That* part you deny."

"Don't be dumb. Someone knew I was going to question the juror. Someone killed him so I couldn't do that. Now, who might that be?"

"How should I know?"

"Because you knew I was going to question him."

"Oh, what, you think I killed him?"

"No, I don't think you killed him. I think someone you told killed him."

"But I didn't tell anyone. I—" Her face froze.

"What is it?"

"Judge Peters saw me looking up the address. He wanted to know what I was doing."

"And you told him the truth?"

"Yes, I told him the truth. I'm not a good liar. And I had his file."

"You had the judge's file?"

"I had the *juror's* file. To look up his address."

"Why did he have a file?"

"He was excused before the completion of the trial. That involved paperwork."

"And his address was in it?"

"That's right."

"This was last night?"

"Right after court. When I went to look it up."

"So you told the judge."

"I *had* to. I'm not the hotshot PI. I'm the dumb blonde who tries to help but can't do anything right."

So. The law clerk was a blonde. That hadn't occurred to me. I thought of her hair as drab and straw-colored.

"Who else did you tell?"

"No one."

"Are you sure?"

"Sure, I'm sure."

"A minute ago you were sure it was no one at all. Now it's no one at all except for the judge."

"Do you think Judge Peters killed the juror?"

"I think he's a better suspect than I am."

"Of course you do. You'll vote for anyone who isn't you."

"I have the advantage of knowing I didn't do it."

I escaped from her clutches, which wasn't easy to do. Before I had the allure of being a private eye. Now I had the added kick of being a murder suspect, and much as the law clerk might profess shock and horror, I got the impression she was actually thrilled. In any event, she wasn't eager to let me go.

I went back in the courtroom, told the bailiff I wanted to see the judge. He didn't argue. I had a feeling the judge wanted to see me.

The judge wasn't eating when I came in. I wondered if it was just too early in the day or if another murder put him off his feed.

"What have you done now?" he said.

I was starting to get a complex. From Thurman to the law clerk to the judge, everyone seemed to think it was my fault.

"I didn't do anything," I said.

"You got a juror killed."

"An ex-juror. It doesn't affect your count."

His mouth fell open. He couldn't believe I'd said that. "How can you joke about a man's death?"

"Sorry. I'm just tired of being blamed for it."

"And yet you caused it."

"Is that how you figure?"

"If you hadn't poked your nose in, would he be alive?"

"How do you know I poked my nose in?"

"You got arrested."

"How do you know that?"

"I'm a judge."

"You have other business. You seem awfully concerned with mine."

"He was one of my jurors."

"Yeah, and you let him go."

"He had a letter from his doctor."

"A letter? You didn't make his doctor come into court?"

"He was the second juror excused. Two jurors is unlucky. Three is getting out of hand."

"I'll remember that."

The judge frowned. "Why are you so angry?"

"I was doing my job and got arrested for it. And everyone seems to blame me. You knew I was doing this. Why didn't you tell me not to?"

"I beg your pardon?"

"Last night. You knew the law clerk was looking up the address. Didn't it strike you as a bad idea then?"

"You'd gone home. It didn't occur to me it would be fatal."

"Me either. I'm upset, and I wanna know what happened."

"Why are you asking me?"

"Because you knew the law clerk looked up the address."

"So?"

"Who'd you tell?"

"I didn't tell anyone."

"You might want to rethink that."

"I beg your pardon."

"Ralph Hogan was killed by someone who knew I was going to question him. It's a very narrow field. It would be wise not to limit it to just you."

The judge straightened in his chair. "Are you accusing me of murder?"

"Not much fun, is it? People have been accusing me all day, I didn't do it, and I'd like to know who did. The law clerk says you're the only one she told. You say you didn't tell anyone. If that's true, we have a problem."

"You have a problem. It's got nothing to do with me."

"Aren't you listening? The suspect list is limited."

"Don't be absurd. You pick a premise, assume it's true, and then get all melodramatic. Someone killed Ralph Hogan. I don't know why, I don't know who. You want to assume it's because of something you did. I can't help it if you're obsessed with guilt. Though I must say, professing guilt at having caused it would be a good way to hide the real guilt of having done it."

"I'm assuming you didn't kill him, Your Honor."

"Generous of you."

"In which case, who'd you tell?"

"I didn't tell anyone."

"A bailiff. A law clerk. An ADA. Your wife."

"I'm not married."

"That would seem to let her out. But anyone else is suspect."

"I didn't tell anyone."

"That's what the law clerk said. Then she remembered she told you."

"And no one else?"

"No."

"Then I wish she hadn't."

"You asked her."

"No, I didn't."

"You caught her looking at the juror's file and asked her what she was doing."

"Yes, because it was late and she should have gone home. "

"And she was holding Ralph Hogan's file."

"If that's what it was. I didn't even notice."

"But she *told* you what it was."

"Yes, she did."

"And she told you I wanted it."

He sighed. "Yes, she did."

"So you knew I was investigating Ralph Hogan. You knew it the night before. And you didn't tell anyone."

Judge Peters scowled. He looked at me distastefully, cocked his head.

"Do you have any friends?"

54

MacAullif looked like he had a bad case of indigestion. "Judge Peters?"

"Yes."

"Your suspect is Judge Peters?"

"I'm afraid so."

"If I had to pick you or Judge Peters, I'd pick you."

"I probably would too."

"But you're not. Instead, you're bursting into a rousing rendition of 'Here Comes the Judge.' Would you care to explain how you think that happened?"

"She was his law clerk. He was hot on her. She dumped him for a negligence lawyer, for Christ's sake."

"Judge Peters?"

"You can't see it?"

"I've seen some pretty unlikely pairings in my day, but Judge Peters and Jeannie Atkins is hard to swallow."

"Because of the difference in their ages?"

"Judge Peters and *anyone* is hard to swallow."

"I'll tell him you said so."

"And if that's the case, what's the deal with number twelve?"

"I don't know."

"You don't know anything. You're flailing around in the dark, grasping at straws."

"I'm not grasping at straws. I'm following leads."

"To the judge? You're following leads to the judge? Granted you've had a bit of a shock, but don't go off the deep end." MacAullif shook his head. "You gonna go hear the testimony?"

"At Richard's trial?"

"Well, not at Judge Peters's. If I were you I'd stay as far the hell away from that as possible."

"I looked in on Richard's trial. Everything was more of the same."

"Which is?"

"Piling on irrelevancies. Witness after witness testifying to things everybody knows. All of which prove he was dating the girl and was in the building that night."

"That's hardly irrelevant."

"They've already proved it, and Richard stipulates it. He says they're just doing it because every time a witness says, 'Richard Rosenberg,' they think he's guilty. He doesn't need me to watch it, and I can't talk to him while it's going on."

"So you thought you'd tell me. Whatsa matter, your wife not home?"

"She's way uptown."

"Ah. The geographic choice. I'm flattered."

"You got any advice? I mean, seriously. Because I haven't got a clue."

"You don't think I was serious? Let me try again. Forget the fucking judge."

My beeper went off. MacAullif rolled his eyes.

I whipped out my cell phone, called the office.

"Stanley," Wendy/Janet said. "Richard wants you to come in right away."

"To the office?"

"Yes."

"Isn't he in court?"

"They rested their case."

55

"Why'd he rest?"

"Jurors were getting bored."

"Oh?"

"Drexler's got better instincts than I thought. I could see it, and he could see it too. Maybe not as quickly as I did."

"How'd you know he wasn't just finished?"

"His witness list. He had more people on it. Cops. Friends. He could have gone on a couple more days. The jurors were getting antsy. And they were happy when I declined to cross-examine. Drexler didn't want me making the jury happy. And like you said, he's already proved his case."

"So why'd you call me in?"

"I thought we might discuss our defense."

"Okay?"

Richard cocked his head. "Is that all you have to say about it?"

"What do you want me to say?"

"Well, I was hoping you'd found a surprise witness who exonerates me."

"'Fraid not."

"So what *have* you got?"

I told him about the judge. He wasn't thrilled.

"Oh, my god. So that's what you've been doing. Trying to solve another murder entirely by pinning it on an elderly jurist with a spotless reputation."

"That's not what I was trying to do."

"No, but it's what you did. That's the stupidest thing I ever heard of."

"That was MacAullif's opinion too."

"You ran this by MacAullif?"

"Yeah."

"Why?"

"You were in court."

"I wasn't in court."

"I didn't know that."

"Not knowing something has never stopped you before." Richard leaned back in his desk chair, rubbed his hand over his forehead. "Well, that sinks it. You think judges don't talk? Wait'll Judge Hollins finds out I'm trying to frame Judge Peters."

"You're not trying to frame Judge Peters."

"That's what it will amount to by the time it reaches him. Things are not going my way. If I can clear you of the murder of this juror, they'll pin it on me. Talk about a conflict of interest."

"You want me to get another lawyer?"

"Good god, no. He'll *actively* try to pin it on me. I don't have to try so hard."

"Just what you want to hear from your lawyer."

234

"Not to win the case. To dangle me as reasonable doubt. So, I can understand your working on your own defense. Did you come up with anything that helps *my* case?"

"We still have the number twelve."

"Oh, my god. I'd forgotten about the number twelve," Richard said sarcastically. "That's it. I'm saved. Oh, wait. That's *your* case again. The juror you killed. Too bad he was long gone when I started dating Jeannie."

"You just started dating her?"

"No. It was a while."

"But not until after this juror got excused?"

"I think so. That shouldn't surprise you. It's been a very long trial."

"Interesting."

"You find that interesting?"

"No. It just seemed the thing to say."

"Forgive me if I've lost my sense of humor. I gotta put on a case tomorrow."

"Tomorrow?"

"That's usually what happens when the prosecution rests."

"Couldn't you get a continuance?"

"I don't want a continuance."

"Why not?"

"Because you killed this juror."

"Richard."

"You know how many times Drexler tried to drag in the Ralph Hogan murder today? It was all I could do to keep it out. And I had Judge Hollins on my side on that one."

"Drexler's trying to poison the jury?"

"Of course he is. I gotta make my case before they all turn against me. Which isn't easy. Not with the *New York Post* screaming JUROR KILLED! on the front page. If you were a juror, would you read that? Nonetheless, it would be better if no one directly attributes it to me."

"You gonna start calling witnesses?"

"Yeah."

"Who you gonna call?"

"Well, that's the thing."

"What?"

"I have no idea."

56

"Richard's really fucked."

Alice was right. I resented her for it. This was not the time for Alice to be right. Not if that's what she thought. If that was her opinion, this was the time for the hundred-to-one shot to come galloping home.

Of course I wouldn't be on it.

I sighed. "What can I do?"

Alice looked at me. "What can *you* do? Are you really as egotistical as that? Richard's going to be convicted, but what can *you* do?"

"What can I do to help *Richard*."

"I got that. Even so, the idea that you have to save him is a little egocentric."

"Someone has to save him. I don't care if it's me. This is a crisis. Someone has to step up."

"You don't think Richard's up to the task?"

"How could he be? He's blinded by the prospect of a guilty verdict."

"So he can't defend himself?"

"He can defend himself. I'm just not sure how well."

"And that is the question, isn't it?" Alice cocked her head. "You think he needs a lawyer?"

My mouth fell open. "Richard?"

"Well, if he can't function under the circumstances."

"He can function."

"You said he had no idea what he's going to do."

"That's what he says. I'm sure he's got something up his sleeve."

"It's not a slip-and-fall, Stanley. It's a murder. His usual intimidation tactics aren't going to cut it."

"You're saying there's nothing he can do?"

"*You're* saying there's nothing he can do. I'm saying hire someone who can."

"I don't think he'd take kindly to the suggestion."

"Kindly? Once again you're worried what he'll think of *you*? I thought your concern was he was in trouble."

"Hiring co-counsel would take time. He'd have to tell the judge his intention and get a continuance while he found a lawyer."

"So?"

"That'll give the prosecution time to poison the jury with Ralph Hogan's murder."

"I thought the judge barred any mention of it."

"He did. But the Hogan murder is in the papers and on TV. The longer Richard takes, the more they're gonna hear about it."

"So, you're washing out all the good work you did with the defense attorneys and the ADAs and the jurors from the Global Bank trial?"

"I'm not washing them out. I just can't use them."

"Why not?"

"I told you, Alice. We gotta steer clear of the dead juror."

"Why, if they're going to see it on TV anyway?"

"There's a difference between seeing it on TV and seeing someone you think did it."

"That's Richard's opinion?"

"It is."

"I think that's a little shortsighted. So what's Richard going to do?"

"He doesn't know."

"He didn't have you subpoena anyone?"

"No."

"That's a bad sign."

"No shit."

"Well, if he doesn't have any witnesses, what *can* he do?"

I shrugged. "Rest his case and proceed to the argument."

Alice stared. "You think he'd do that?"

"He's unconventional. He skipped voire dire empaneling the jury."

"That's different. This would be a tremendous gamble."

"I know."

"If he rested right now, what would the jury do?"

"Find him guilty. Unless he made one hell of an argument."

"What could he say?"

"'I didn't do it. I can't prove it, but take my word for it.'"

"Hmmm," Alice said. "Probably a bad idea."

"I would think."

Alice thought that over. "So, Richard flies in the face of conventional wisdom, right?"

"Right."

"And conventional wisdom says keep the dead juror out of it?"

"What are you saying?"

The phone rang. I grabbed it off the wall.

It was Richard. "Stanley. Stop by the office tomorrow morning before court."

"Sure. Why?"

"I want you to serve a subpoena."

57

Court was dull. Oh, not Richard's. The Global Banking case. When I pushed my way through the door, the ADA was cross-examining one of the defense witnesses. No one was thrilled. He'd been cross-examining him the day before. Even the lawyers' objections seemed tired and listless, like they were just going through the motions.

My confidante, the law clerk who fancied herself a dumb blonde, pushed from her seat and tried to head me off. I brushed by her, headed up the aisle.

Judge Peters glanced up and saw me. I was clearly the last person in the world he wanted to see. I hoped my distraction didn't make him miss some of the riveting testimony.

There was an empty seat on the aisle, right near the front. I ignored it, pushed through the gate. Before anyone could stop me I walked right between the defense and prosecution tables, headed for the witness stand.

Something in the witness's face made the ADA turn. He saw me and gawked.

I strode up to him and said, "Mr. Edelstein. You're subpoenaed to testify for the defense in the case of the *People vs. Rosenberg* this afternoon at two o'clock."

This happened fast.

The judge banged the gavel and shouted, "Bailiff!"

He needn't have bothered. The bailiff and a court officer were already converging on me. They grabbed me, spun me around, wrestled my arms behind my back.

"Mr. Hastings. You're in contempt of court. This little stunt will cost you two thousand dollars and five days in jail."

"Yes, Your Honor," I said. "But unless you want to adjourn for the day, ADA Edelstein better brief his associate on what he planned for the afternoon."

Judge Peters looked furious. He banged the gavel. "Court's in recess for half an hour. Bring him to my chambers."

The bailiff and court officer wrestled me in.

"That will do," Judge Peters said, and they withdrew.

"They didn't take off the handcuffs," I said.

"All right. What do you think you're doing?"

"I'm working for the defense attorney in a murder trial. He told me to serve a subpoena."

"And you had to do it in open court?"

"Someone had to do something. The witness was boring."

"That fine can be increased."

"Bad idea. You'll just look spiteful."

Judge Peters controlled himself with an effort. "Would you mind telling me what this is all about?"

"The prosecution rested. When Richard starts calling witnesses, ADA Drexler plans to drag in the Ralph Hogan murder on cross-examination. Richard figures he will if there's any testimony about this case."

"So he subpoenas the prosecutor?"

"It could be worse."

"How could it be worse?"

"He could have subpoenaed you."

Judge Peters exhaled. "Would you like to keep your two thousand dollars and not go to jail?"

"That might interest me."

"Would you mind telling me why Richard Rosenberg has subpoenaed the prosecutor as his witness?"

I shrugged. "Frankly, Your Honor, I don't think he has anyone else."

58

I got to see it. Not that the judge was buyin' the bullshit, or anything, but he agreed to hold off my incarceration until the completion of Richard's trial. I think he just didn't want to give Richard ground for appeal by depriving him of his investigator during defense testimony, though whether that would be ground for appeal, I have no idea. But then Richard can argue anything.

ADA Edelstein looked as happy as a drowned rat. I don't know why that image came to me. He wasn't wet in the least, wasn't sweating his testimony. He just looked pissed. He was sworn in and took the stand.

Richard walked up to him and smiled. "Mr. Edelstein, do you know me?"

"I don't know you personally. I know who you are."

"And I know who you are. It's nice to actually meet. I understand we have something in common."

The ADA's eyes narrowed. His look was guarded. "What do you mean?"

"Well, we're both attorneys," Richard said. "You are currently the prosecutor in the Global Banking case?"

"You should know. You subpoenaed me off of it."

"Yes. Sorry about that. But I'm also the defendant in this action. That isn't the case in your trial, is it? I mean, you're not prosecuting yourself?"

"Objection, Your Honor. Does the defense attorney have any questions for this witness or was subpoenaing him abuse of process?"

"Sustained. Mr. Rosenberg, could you confine yourself to relevant questions?"

"Yes, Your Honor. Mr. Edelstein, the Global Banking case that you are prosecuting has been going on for several weeks, has it not?"

"It certainly has."

"And the decedent was a law clerk for Judge Peters, who is presiding in that case."

"Yes, she was."

"Did you know her?"

"I had seen her in court. I knew who she was."

"Lots of people saw her in court and knew who she was. Did you have a personal relationship with the decedent?"

"I had spoken to her."

Richard smiled. "You are clearly an attorney. Your answers, while not lies, evade the question. I asked you if you had a *personal* relationship with her. Since you take that to mean speaking, let me ask, did you have an *intimate* relationship with her?"

"Objection."

"Overruled."

ADA Edelstein looked uncomfortable. He cleared his throat. "I had seen her once or twice."

Richard smiled again. "*Personal* you take to mean talking. *Intimate* you take to mean seeing. Let's find out what you take *sexual* to mean. Did you have a *sexual* relationship with her?"

"Objection. Already asked and answered."

"Overruled."

"Did you have a sexual relationship with Jeannie Atkins?"

"Yes, but it was very brief."

"Had you been up to her apartment?"

"Yes."

"Did you have a key?"

"For a brief period of time."

"Define *brief*."

"I suppose a few weeks. I can't remember."

"And was it during the time I was dating Jeannie Atkins?"

"I don't know when you were dating Jeannie Atkins."

"I was dating her when she died."

"It wasn't then."

"You had ended the relationship before then?"

"Yes."

"But it was during the trial?"

"Yes, but it's been a long trial."

"Really? You must not be very good at it. This one's going quite quickly."

The gavel came down. "Mr. Rosenberg, I've warned you about such side comments."

"Sorry, Your Honor. Mr. Edelstein, you claim you had a key to the decedent's apartment?"

"Yes. For a short time."

"So you gave it back to her?"

"That's right."

"Did you give it back to her personally?"

"I left it in her apartment."

"When did you do that?"

"When I realized the relationship was finished."

"You didn't tell her the relationship was finished, you just left the key in her apartment?"

"I didn't want to make a scene."

"And when did this happen?"

"I don't recall."

"How many days before her death?"

"I don't remember."

"It was *before* her death, wasn't it, that you left your key in her apartment?"

"I resent that!"

"You resent the murder implication? How do you think I feel?"

"Mr. Rosenberg."

"Sorry, Your Honor, but the witness did not answer the question. He said he resented it, but he didn't answer it." Richard turned back to the witness. "You left your key in Jeannie Atkins's apartment *before* she died?"

"Yes."

"Thank you. That's all."

ADA Drexler could hardly wait to get at the witness. "Mr. Edelstein, you are the prosecutor for the Global Banking case?"

"That's right."

"And Jeannie Atkins was a law clerk for Judge Peters, who is presiding?"

"That's correct."

"That case has been going on for several weeks?"

"Months, now."

"Is the jury sequestered?"

Richard sprang to his feet. "Objection, Your Honor. Relevance."

"Counsel brought out the fact the witness is the prosecutor in the Global Banking case, and he and the decedent met during the course of that trial. I should be allowed to examine the circumstances of that meeting."

"Overruled."

"The jury is not sequestered."

"To your knowledge, did some of Jeannie Atkins's duties have to do with the jury?"

"Yes. She ran errands, ordered the meals."

"Were any of the jurors replaced during the course of that trial?"

"Yes. We had four alternates. Two jurors were replaced. We have only two alternates left."

"The jurors that were replaced. Do you know their names?"

"I know one of their names. Ralph Hogan."

"How do you know his name?"

"I didn't know it during the course of the trial, but I know it now."

"Why is that?"

"He was murdered over the weekend. Mr. Rosenberg's investigator was arrested at the scene of the crime."

There was a startled gasp from the courtroom.

Judge Hollins looked expectantly at the defense table. Richard said nothing, sat quietly. He didn't seem to be paying attention.

"Mr. Rosenberg."

"Yes, Your Honor."

"Did you hear the last question and answer?"

"Yes, Your Honor."

"Do you wish to object to it?"

"Are you running my case for me, Your Honor?"

"I do not wish to be overturned on the grounds you were not given an opportunity to object because you were distracted and did not hear the question."

"I heard the question, Your Honor, and the answer. I'm not going to object to things that are indisputable."

"Very well. Proceed, Mr. Drexler."

ADA Drexler smiled. "Thank you, Your Honor. No further questions."

ADA Edelstein got up to leave the witness stand.

Richard held up his hand. "Excuse me. I have one or two questions on redirect." He approached the witness. "Ralph Hogan?"

"I beg your pardon?"

"You say the name of the juror who was killed was Ralph Hogan?"

"That's right."

"That's the name of the juror who was discovered murdered in his apartment by my investigator?"

"I didn't say he was discovered by your investigator. I said your investigator was *arrested* in his apartment."

"Let's not quibble. That's the name of the juror on your jury who was replaced and subsequently killed?"

"That's right."

"But you didn't know his name during the course of the trial?"

"No."

"And how is that?"

"During the course of the trial, the jurors are referred to by the numbers of their seats. Unless you have a photographic memory—which I do not—and remember from voir dire, there is no reason an ADA would know a juror's name."

"I see. And what number was Ralph Hogan?"

"I don't recall."

"Really? Once you saw his picture in the paper, and realized he'd been killed, didn't you visualize him sitting in the jury box? Didn't you recall the person who filled his position? Didn't you recall what position that was?"

The ADA exhaled. "When you put it that way, I can work it out. It was juror twelve."

"Thank you." Richard picked up a plastic evidence bag from the defense table. "Your Honor, I ask that this be marked for identification as Defendant's Exhibit A."

"So ordered."

When the exhibit had been marked, Richard took it and approached the witness. "Mr. Edelstein, I hand you an evidence bag marked for identification as Defendant's Exhibit A and ask you what you see inside."

"It's a small piece of paper."

"Is there anything written on that paper?"

"The numeral 12 is printed on it."

"That's right. And have you ever seen that piece of paper before?"

"No, I have not."

"Really? Is it not true that you saw it when you left it for Jeannie Atkins to find as part of a prearranged plan? Is it not true that in addition to being Jeannie Atkins's lover you were also her co-conspirator, that you conspired with her to replace certain members of the jury who were sympathetic to the defense? Is it not a fact that you struck up a relationship with Jeannie Atkins primarily for the purpose of gaining insight into the jurors' perspective? That after you had gotten her totally infatuated, you persuaded her to help you influence certain jurors to leave the jury, either through bribes or inducements or promise of sexual favors or blackmail or extortion or some combination or other?"

"Objection, Your Honor!" ADA Drexler began.

Richard cut him off with a voice of steel. "I have not yet finished my question. You hold your objection until I am done." He raised his voice to drown out any further interruption. "Is it not true, Mr. Edelstein, that once you had Jeannie Atkins totally entangled in your plot, you entered into a relationship with a defense attorney on the very case you were handling, and while you had to keep that relationship secret, you could not keep it secret from the decedent? Is it not true that the defense attorney was the jealous type, forcing you to sever all relations with Jeannie Atkins? Despite this, you and Jeannie Atkins were still carrying out your plot, and since you could not be seen with her, you conspired to leave messages for her. You left this paper with the number twelve for Jeannie Atkins to find, telling her to replace defense-friendly juror Ralph Hogan. You expected her to destroy the paper, never guessing that she would become so nervous about what she had done that she would hang on to this paper for safekeeping in case she was ever called on to account for her actions. And is it not true that after she began dating me, Jeannie Atkins became so consumed with guilt over what she had done that she went to you, told you she could not live with herself, that she planned to confess her sins and throw herself on the mercy of the court? You managed to stall her along, promising to meet her the next day, but instead you lay in wait outside her apartment building the night of the crime. You saw me leave at eleven fifteen, not eleven forty-five, as has been testified by a driver eager to justify his padded overtime charges and a doorman eager to cover up the fact he actually locked the front door and went home early. You entered Jeannie Atkins's apartment building at eleven thirty after the doorman left and before the super replaced him on the desk, using the key that Jeannie Atkins had given you and you had not yet given back. Under the guise of pretending to talk to her about the confession she wished to make, you contrived to obtain a steak knife from the kitchen and stab her to death in her bed, tearing off and bearing away the flimsy negligee she was wearing so it would look like she was killed while she was nude."

Richard stabbed a finger in the witness's face. "Is that not a fact, Mr. Edelstein?"

"Objection!" Drexler thundered.

And the court went wild.

59

Judge Peters poured Richard a brandy. He looked over at me.

"He doesn't drink," Richard said.

The judge nodded. "Good. Nasty habit." He poured himself one and settled back in his chair. "So, you have successfully destroyed my case. It's a mistrial, any way you slice it. Even if ADA Edelstein isn't charged with the murder, the jury tampering alone would be grounds."

"I would point out that all that happened before my trial had even begun," Richard said.

"Yes, but who would have known?"

"Your Honor!"

"Oh, don't Your Honor me. We're drinking brandy here. I am not saying on or off the record I would want a trial to proceed despite such an irregularity. "

"And isn't the ADA dating the defense attorney enough for a mistrial?" I pointed out.

"That is yet to be proved. There's no real evidence, unless someone talks."

"Ah, well," Richard said. "Things don't always work out."

"Easy for you to say. You got a dismissal."

"I'd have preferred an acquittal," Richard said. "With a dismissal some moron ADA could decide to charge me again."

"I doubt that will happen," Judge Peters said. "They can't prosecute you *and* him."

"He may be hard to convict. He is, after all, an ADA."

"That's no shield to prosecution."

"We lawyers are a sneaky bunch."

"What will happen with your case?" I said.

The judge shrugged. "It's a mistrial. A prosecutor could refile, but it certainly won't be him. And with the amount of pretrial work just sifting through these transcripts, it's going to be a while before anything gets on the docket. And all the while, accounts are being manipulated, monies are being hid. I'd hate to have to sort that out."

"If they did retry it, would you have to preside?" I said.

"Oh, yes," he said dryly. "It's not like you got me out of anything. Just doubled my pleasure, doubled my fun. Can you imagine listening to that testimony a second time? Ruling on those same objections? At least I won't have your shiny face haunting the trial. Pestering the jurors." He shook his head. "I can't believe ADA Edelstein killed that juror."

"I'm sure you were perfectly happy to believe I did," Richard said.

"You were a much more likely suspect."

"Why? No one had the faintest idea this juror even existed. Why would I look him up just to kill him?"

"Suppose he looked you up?"

Richard considered that. "Blackmail?"

"Sure."

"And what would Ralph Hogan blackmail me for?"

"Killing Jeannie Atkins."

"How would he know? What proof could he offer?"

"None," I said, "since Richard didn't do it. Even if he had, what's the connection? The juror was long gone before the murder. What could he possibly know about it?"

"Obviously he couldn't. But Richard wasn't being tried for Ralph Hogan's murder. All ADA Drexler had to do was tarnish him with innuendo. Just as he attempted."

"That didn't work out so well," I said.

"Not at all. A most ingenious defense, Mr. Rosenberg. It's not every day you can decide the outcome of two trials with one witness." The judge chuckled.

"What's so funny, Your Honor?" Richard said.

"ADA Drexler. Charging you with abuse of process. It would be hard to imagine a more relevant witness."

60

Postmortem number two took place without Judge Peters. I preferred that. The guy wasn't charging me with contempt of court anymore, but I still found his presence inhibiting.

We also conducted it without the presence of Wendy and Janet, which was not easy, as they were eager to congratulate Richard on his victory. It was all we could do make it through the outer office.

"That's the most amazing thing I've ever seen," I said, when we were safely ensconced in Richard's office. "Did you have that whole incredible summation mapped out yesterday when you asked me to serve that subpoena?"

"Good lord, no. I just figured I'd get him on the stand and accuse him of murder."

"And then you figured out how he did it."

"Well, that's one way to look at it."

"What do you mean?"

"I figured out how he *could* have done it. Doesn't mean I was right."

"Maybe not every detail, but you certainly got the gist. Did you see the guy's face? The jury could convict him just on that."

Richard shrugged. "Well, we know they don't need evidence."

"But the way you laid it out. It made such perfect sense. I felt stupid for not seeing it before."

"Don't be silly."

"You even accounted for the key."

Richard frowned. "What key?"

"The key Sergeant Thurman asked about. The police found it in the apartment, figured it was yours. That's why Thurman wanted me to find out if you had a key."

"I don't think so."

"What do you mean, you don't think so? That was part of your theory. ADA Edelstein let himself in with a key and left it in the apartment. The police found it there and thought it was yours."

Richard shook his head. "No, they didn't."

"What do you mean, 'no, they didn't?'"

"Stanley, just because a lawyer asks a question doesn't make it true. Yes, I asked him if he let himself in with a key and left it in her apartment, because it made the story sound better. That doesn't mean it happened."

"You mean it was *your* key the police found there?"

"No."

"How can you be sure?"

Richard reached in his pocket, pulled out a key ring with a single key. "Because I have it right here."

My eyes widened. "Then it *was* Edelstein's key."

"No, it wasn't."

"Richard."

"There was only one key. Jeannie got it *back* from him and gave it to me."

"He didn't *have* a key?"

"No."

"Then how'd he get into the apartment?"

Richard shrugged. "Your guess is as good as mine."

"Then how could he commit the crime?"

"Once again, I can't help you with that."

"Richard, you accused him of murder."

"Yeah, but they can't find him guilty on my say-so. They can't even make me testify against him. Because I don't know anything. All of that's conjecture. I have plausible deniability up and down the line."

"But he's going to trial. And he may not have done it."

"That's no bar to prosecution. Look at me."

"How can you let that happen?"

"How can I stop it? For all I know, he did it. I don't *know* he did. I just know I didn't. And if somebody's gotta sweat out the prosecution, I'd prefer it was him."

I slumped back in the big client's chair and rubbed my eyes. "So it was just a stunt. What about the number twelve?"

"I think it's a reasonable explanation."

"But if you're right, the ADA killed Ralph Hogan to cover it up."

"Yeah."

"How'd he know I was going to see him? How'd he know the guy was a threat?"

"The law clerk knew. The judge knew. Why not an ADA?"

"The judge found out by seeing the law clerk."

"And the ADA couldn't have seen her?"

"How?"

"I don't know. Didn't she think she was playing spy?"

I blinked. "Yes, she did."

61

My confidante couldn't believe I was calling her. The case was over, so it had to be personal. Her voice quivered in anticipation.

She met me at a coffee shop on Broadway. I could tell she was disappointed. She was hoping to lure me up to her apartment. She'd dressed slinky, which was hard to take. Her slacks were tight, her sweater clung. She'd fluffed up her blond hair. It cascaded down her neck, rather than hanging limply. I felt sorry for her, dolling herself up for a middle-aged man.

I'd gotten her number from Judge Peters. He hadn't been pleased to see me, commented that it was the second time in one day. I pointed out it was the third time, if you counted the subpoena. Probably a gutsy move.

"This is so nice," she said. "I didn't expect to see you now that the trial is over."

"I guess it's just fate."

Her eyes gleamed. "You think so?"

"Could be."

"So," she said. "What'd you have in mind?"

"I thought we'd start with coffee. Want a latte?"

"Sure," she said, though I could tell that wasn't what she had in mind.

I bought a pair of lattes, took them to a table in the corner. We sat, had a sip.

"I need your help with the case," I said.

That was the last thing she wanted to hear. Disappointment flooded her face. "The case is over."

"I mean the Rosenberg case."

"They dismissed it."

"Yes. And now they're charging the ADA."

"I can't believe he did it."

"I can't either," I said.

Her eyes narrowed. The playful quality was gone. "What do you mean?"

"Richard made a good case against him, but there's holes in it. We gotta be sure he's convicted. If he isn't convicted, they could still turn around and charge Richard at some later date."

"They wouldn't do that."

"It's the law. You don't say that would never happen. You say I need to make sure it *couldn't* happen. An acquittal would have been a bar to future prosecution. A dismissal isn't."

"Yes, but—"

"So we gotta dot the i's and cross the t's. Edelstein looks good for it. They should be able to get a conviction. But as you know, a defense attorney can argue anything. And some fool juror will think there's reasonable doubt."

"So?"

"The problem is Ralph Hogan. He's the hole in the story. No one knew I was calling on Ralph Hogan. I knew it, and you knew it, and Richard knew it. And Judge Peters saw you looking it up, so he could have known it. But he claims he didn't tell anyone, and I don't know why he'd lie. Which leaves you."

"I wouldn't lie either."

"But somewhere, between the time you got the address and the time I went to the apartment, ADA Edelstein had to have learned I was going to do it. If there's no way he could have found out, that's a huge hole in the prosecution's case. You could help me out with that."

"You think I told someone?"

"That's the only explanation."

"I didn't."

"Your lips say no, no, no, but your eyes say yes, yes, yes."

She frowned. "What?"

"You claim you never told ADA Edelstein. That's a lie. I think you were sweet on ADA Edelstein and seized every moment to ingratiate yourself. Which doesn't really surprise me. You're not the first woman to have two-timed me."

"How can you say that?"

"Well, ADA Edelstein is a lot younger than I am, and he's single. He's a far more promising catch. I'm just a private eye flirtation. A storybook romance of no consequence. I think your infatuation with the ADA is the real thing. So I can understand your covering for him. What could be more romantic than saving him from a murder conviction? But you are covering for him, and eventually it's going to come out. And the sooner it does, the easier it'll go on you."

She hesitated, bit her lip.

"It's not like they won't get him anyway. As soon as they realize Rosenberg couldn't have done it—"

"All right, I told him."

"When?"

"After court. I caught up with him on his way to the subway. I thought he'd be glad to hear it. I thought he'd be grateful."

"He wasn't?"

"He was angry. For telling him. As if it was my fault."

"Don't shoot the messenger."

"But I can't believe he did anything. I still think Rosenberg did it."

"Yeah. You kind of have to say that."

"What do you mean?"

I smiled, then shook my head pityingly. "You didn't see Edelstein after court. He'd already gone home. I watched him go. Actually rode uptown with him. Which is how I know he didn't see you at all. You made that up. It was what you needed me to hear."

"I don't know what you're talking about."

"Yeah, you do. And you know what it means. This is your last chance. If you insist you saw him after court, you're caught in a lie that can be proven false. Nothing can save you then."

She opened her mouth, closed it. Swayed slightly.

MacAullif heaved himself to his feet at the table next to ours. The good sergeant was wired on coffee. He'd been waiting for some time. He marched up to our table, clapped handcuffs on my confidante's wrists, and began reciting Miranda.

The poor girl looked like she'd been punched in the stomach. I kept quiet while MacAullif droned on. It was quite a while. When he'd finished Mirandizing her for the Ralph Hogan murder, he turned around and went through the whole spiel again for Jeannie Atkins.

Somewhere in there she fainted.

62

Richard was offended. "You might have told me what you were going to do."

"I thought you might stop me."

"Why would I stop you when you're right?"

"How would you know I'm right?"

"You think I wouldn't know?"

"I don't know how. I didn't."

"It was all a bluff?"

"Just like your cross-examination of ADA Edelstein."

"Yeah, but that had the advantage of being total bullshit."

"So was mine. I didn't ride home on the subway with Edelstein. I left way before he did. But she didn't know that. She thought I'd caught her in a lie."

"That's a harmless deception. I'm talking pure fiction. A conspiracy to remove jurors, for Christ's sake."

"I thought you liked that theory."

"I like any theory that gets me off the hook, but get real. An ADA asks a law clerk to bounce jurors off a panel for him? What courtroom thriller did you rip that off from?"

"But—"

"But what?"

"The envelope taped to the bottom of her panties drawer."

Richard smiled wistfully. "Jeannie didn't have a lot of money. But she liked to have some on hand, just in case. And not in her purse, which she could lose or someone could steal. She wanted an emergency stash at home. I never asked where she kept it."

"There wasn't any money in the envelope, Richard."

He shrugged. "She either spent it or the killer stole it."

"What about the number twelve?"

"Ah, yes. The cryptic clue." Richard cocked his head. "Did you measure the envelope?"

"Huh?"

"The manila envelope. Measure the envelope. No, don't bother, I already did. It's a twelve-inch envelope. If you find the store that sold it, I bet they have ten-inch envelopes, and at least one of them will have a little ten in it."

"Son of a bitch."

The phone rang.

Richard scooped it up. "I said no calls . . . Oh . . . Send him in."

Sergeant MacAullif pushed his way into the room, pulled up the nearest chair, flopped himself down. "Girls didn't want to call you. I had to get rough."

"I gathered," Richard said. "What's up?"

"She's confessing."

"I'm not surprised," I said.

MacAullif cocked his head ironically. "Of course not. Now that it's happened, you predict it."

"I mean she's the type to confess. A depressed, lonely woman, living out a storybook existence, fancying herself the heroine in some noir movie, melodramatically taking the fall for her lover."

MacAullif shrugged. "Or she saw she was trapped and hoped to get a better deal."

"If she's confessing, why are you here?" Richard said.

"They kicked me out. Not my case. It's Thurman's case. He and the ADA are having a go at her."

"Any details?"

"They told her she had the right to an attorney. She named ADA Edelstein. You can imagine how thrilled he was. He was still in custody at the time. And she lied to the police and implicated him in the Ralph Hogan murder. He turned her down hard. That's when she had a fit of remorse and threw herself in front of a bus."

"How are you getting this?"

MacAullif shrugged. "Some cops don't like Thurman much. Some ADAs too. And I'd made the arrest." He stuck his finger in my face. "And you're not quoting me on that."

"Not even to the *Post*?"

"Fuck you."

"What else you got?" Richard said.

"She killed Jeannie Atkins out of jealousy. For trying to steal her beloved ADA."

"But they weren't an item anymore. He'd moved on."

"Yeah, but there was a conspiracy too," MacAullif said. "I understand you brought it out in court. About removing jurors."

"What's that got to do with anything?"

"She said it was a big misunderstanding. Tragic irony, that's the word coming out of the interrogation room. Apparently she actually said it. ADA Edelstein found out one of the jurors was prodefense and wanted him replaced. Managed to get Jeannie alone to tell her.

Our girl saw it and flipped out. That slut! Going out with you and still making a play for him. She hacks her up with a steak knife. Probably enjoyed doing it."

Richard chuckled, shook his head. "Bullshit upon bullshit."

"What's that?" MacAullif said.

"I make up some ridiculous story just trying to raise reasonable doubt, and everybody runs with it. There is no evidence whatsoever that ADA Edelstein was involved in a clandestine scheme to replace jurors. If the guy pulled Jeannie aside the day she was killed, most likely he was just trying to hit on her."

"Maybe," MacAullif said. "But some of the details are probably true. She watched you leave, sailed right through the lobby while the doorman was dealing with some delivery boy. So they got her dead to rights. Even if they don't, they certainly won't be hassling you."

"What about Ralph Hogan?" I said. "She copping to that too?"

"Oh, sure. When she caved she went whole hog."

"And why did she kill him?"

"She was afraid he'd implicate the ADA in jury tampering. At least that's what she claims now that she's trying to protect the guy. Speculation is she was pissed off at him for making a pass at Jeannie and did it to spite him. Planned to let it slip ever so reluctantly that she'd told him you were going to question Hogan, so we'd think he killed him to save himself."

"What's happening with ADA Edelstein?"

"I think they let him go. They figure he wasn't an accessory to the murder, and no one's very interested in trying him for jury tampering. The bar association may have something to say about it, but it's an iffy criminal case."

"Considering it's total bullshit," Richard said.

"Anyway, happy ending," MacAullif said.

Richard's smile froze on his face. He blinked once, said flatly, "Yeah."

"Sorry. She meant something to you, didn't she?" MacAullif exhaled. "Well, I thought you'd want to hear the update."

"Thanks."

There was an uncomfortable silence.

MacAullif got out of there as fast as he could without making it look like he was fleeing. Or at least he tried to. It sure looked that way to me.

I don't know what it looked like to Richard. He wasn't really paying attention. He'd slipped into a kind of netherworld, overwhelmed by it all, the case suddenly over, if not solved at least figured out, or as figured out as it was likely to get, with all the principals either dead or lying.

I left shortly after that. I don't even recall what I said, I just remember how he looked.

He was tipped back in his desk chair, his top button unbuttoned and his tie pulled down, his eyes cloudy, dazed, like a battered and beaten prizefighter, but misted over too, as if on the verge of forming teardrops, just an old brokenhearted lawyer with a fool for a client.